THE GATHERING

The Crossroads Trilogy
Book One

Kara Stalnaker

Kardee's Angel Publishing

Kardee's Angel Publishing
Tobaccoville, NC 27050

www.kardeesangelpublishing.com

TABLE OF CONTENTS

DEDICATION

I would like to thank first and foremost God for being part of my everyday life and always being there for me. You guide my life in the way you would have me live it and I always treasure your guidance.

I would also like to thank my family: My mom, dad, and my sister and her family. Thank you for always being so understanding and always being there for me. I love you all.

PROLOGUE

In the beginning, God created the Heaven and the Earth. Light pierced the dark skies as it slowly created a shadow that was cast upon the darkness. Light and darkness fought to remain over a period of time, slowly turning into night and day. In Heaven, the realm however was not so quiet or at peace. Through the shadows an angel lurked. His beauty matched with his strength. He was among the highest ranked angels, such as Michael and Gabriel, who were chosen as leaders among the angel armies. He watched quietly from the shadows as Michael and Gabriel listened to God's words at the throne. Michael looked back over his broad shoulder at the presence of an angel named Lucifer who continued to watch silently. "Come forward," Michael called in a demanding voice as he turned to him. Michael always had his sword at his side and was heavily armed at all times. His voice echoed through the golden halls. Gabriel glanced back; his sparkling blue eyes and spotless pale skin gave away his youthful characteristics. Lucifer moved forward, slowly staring down at the brick walkway. His golden garments sparkled brightly in the light. "What is it?" Michael asked.

Lucifer looked up at him. "I wish to speak to our Father," he said. Michael stepped down the marble steps and waited allowing Lucifer to speak to God. Lucifer stepped up to the bright golden light and smiled. "Father, I wish to speak to you," he said kneeling. He looked up at the light. "I can help you, we can be as one," he whispered. Michael and Gabriel watched silently, surprised by the words that came from Lucifer. No angel had ever brought that type of conversation up with God. It was forbidden among the angels to speak to their father in such a way. "You must give me a chance! I can be like you, we all can!" Lucifer called. "I have many that will follow," he continued, kneeling down and touching the light with his impure hands. The light suddenly grew wide as Lucifer fell backwards and slid down the steps. Michael and Gabriel walked up to Lucifer, as God grew angry at the betrayal of one of his creations. They watched the light and nodded, knowing what they were ordered to do. Michael and Gabriel snatched Lucifer's arms and yanked him back.

"You can't do this!" he shouted. "They will follow us!" he called as he's pulled away from the steps.

Lucifer broke free and raced up the steps. "Please!" he begged, getting on his knees. Michael and Gabriel were already at his side. They pulled him back. Anger had now overcome Lucifer. "If you do this, you will regret it!" he shouted. "I will hunt down everything you create. I will destroy everything and make them suffer!" he shouted as they dragged him from sight.

Michael and Gabriel forced Lucifer to the ground outside the gates of Heaven. Lucifer looked back at them in anger. "I don't understand this!" he called. "You are my brothers!" Michael pulled the sword from the sheath on his belt. Lucifer sunk back in fear as he stared at the blade. "You wouldn't!" he called. Michael slammed the sword to the ground. A crack of thunder could be heard as Lucifer stood. "This isn't over, my brother!" he called as he disappeared into the darkness. Michael and Gabriel watched silently knowing what they did was the will of God.

Lucifer lay on the hard packed sand. Slowly he lifted his head and looked around the desert region that he had been sent to. Rising, he saw those that followed him rise. They rose and looked around in fear, seeing nothing but darkness and desert all around them. "Our Father has abandoned us!" Lucifer called to them. He glanced over at the hills and saw hundreds of angels standing and watching silently, betrayed by their brother.

Michael and Gabriel stood, watching from the hillside, while thousands of angels stood behind them. "You are no longer able to return," Michael called.

"Our Father has abandoned me!" Lucifer shouted in anger. Gabriel looked over at Michael. He nodded slowly and walked away as Michael pulled out his sword and pressed it down in the sand. The sand began to boil as it turned into red and orange lava. The lava spread around Lucifer and his angels. Lucifer looked back at Michael and smiled. "I will see you again, brother!" he shouted as steam came up around him.

"We will meet again, brother, on this battlefield," Michael snapped as the angels around him backed away. Michael continued to watch as lava spread around Lucifer. He and his angels disappeared into the flames and steam coming from the lava. Slowly Michael walked away as a low laugh could be heard from the fire.

CHAPTER ONE

Victor, a local police officer in his mid thirties, sat in the stands with his adoptive parents, watching his younger brother Gabriel who was in his late teens, walk up to bat at the local baseball game. "Go Gabe!" he shouted, clapping as Gabriel tapped the plate with the metal bat and positioned the bat as he watched the pitcher in front of him. The pitcher threw the ball. The ball snapped from the metal bat and flew across the field at neck breaking speed and went over the fence. The crowd, including Victor and his parents, were on their feet, cheering, as Gabriel raced from plate to plate. This was his third home run in the game. Victor smiled and clapped as Gabriel walked over to the dugout and took a seat on the bench. Several players slapped him a high five, in honor of putting them ahead.After the game, Victor waited beside the car with his parents as Gabriel walked out with a trophy. "Oh sweetheart, you did great!" Jackie said, hugging him. Gabriel smiled, as he handed his bag to his father.

"Look at you, mister, you hit the ball out of the park three times!" Victor said. Gabriel smiled but remained silent. He hadn't spoken a word since they were adopted. Their adopted parents had been told that Gabriel had been traumatized from the death of their biological parents, but there was never any record of them, or their death, in the police database.

"This calls for some pizza on the way home!" Jackie said. Her husband smiled and nodded as they walked over to the car. Victor watched his brother.

"They could be worse, you know," he said as Gabriel looked over at him. "I know, it's not home, but we're okay," Victor added. "Good job today," he said hugging his brother tightly. "Now go, enjoy the pizza," he said pushing him on to the car. Gabriel looked back at him. "Go! Go celebrate! I'll be by the house later," Victor said. He watched as his brother walked over to the car and got in. He sighed as he glanced back at the woods close by and saw Jared standing at the edge of the woods. Jared was a close friend of Victor for many years. He had dark hair and tanned skin. He often stayed out of sight, but often visited Michael when something important came up. Jared watched him as Victor walked over to him. Victor leaned against the tree. "What do you have?" Victor asked as Jared held up a picture. Victor took the picture and examined it. The picture showed a man stepping down from the plane. The man in the photo was surrounded by several guards protecting him from the hoards of people that had showed up to meet him.

"He's making his move," Jared said as Victor looked down at the picture. "His name is Mason. He's been talked about for several months now," Jared continued.

"That means the rapture will happen soon, he'll wait till the rapture happens to come into power," Victor said. Victor handed the picture back to Jared. "Keep me informed," he said. Jared nodded as he retreated to the woods and disappeared. Victor walked from the woods and over to his patrol car and got in.

On the way home Gabriel sat in the back seat of his parent's vehicle with a smile as he stared at the trophy in the seat. "We're proud of you," his mother said. Gabriel smiled as he looked at her then back at the trophy. They pulled up to the stoplight and waited at the four-way intersection. The light finally turned green as Gabriel's father started to cross the intersection. "Look out!" his mother screamed. A car sped through the intersection slamming into the side of the car causing it to roll violently several times and coming to a stop on its hood. Steam slowly rose from the vehicle, as everything remained still and quiet.

Victor sat in the driver's seat of his patrol car as he headed back towards the station. "We got a two car accident, reporting multiple casualties," the dispatched announced over the radio. Victor groaned and turned on the sirens as he sped towards the scene. He was the first to arrive at the scene and stopped. He got out quickly seeing the metal and glass shattered across the intersection. It looked as though a bomb had gone off. Racing over to the first car he reached in and felt the driver's neck. He groaned not feeling a pulse. He raced over towards the other car and gasped as he saw that it was his parent's car. He raced over frantically and knelt down.

"Mom! Dad!" He shouted looking into the car. People from the other cars were racing around the scene trying to find ways to help. He reached in and felt his mother's neck for a pulse. He slowly lowered his head not feeling one. He could see his father in the driver's seat and could tell there was no hope for him, as he saw the large amount of blood coming from the gash in his forehead. Glancing back into the back seat he could see Gabriel lying motionless on glass and tangled metal. "Gabe?" he whispered. He slid to the back of the car and reached in through the shattered window. He felt his brother's neck and couldn't feel a pulse. Taking out his baton he cleared out the rest of the shattered glass. He reached back in and felt again. There was blood all around. Glancing back he saw the people helping but not paying attention to him. Looking back at his brother, he shut his eyes as he placed his hand on his neck that had been possibly broken. He opened his eyes and felt for a pulse again. There was now a weak pulse. Victor glanced back as an ambulance arrived. "I need help over here!" He called. Several paramedics raced over. "This is my family!" Victor said as he backed away slowly. He watched the paramedics take over. He glanced over as Jared stood at the edge of the forest watching. Slowly he walked back into the woods and disappeared.

At the hospital, Victor sat waiting quietly. The clock ticked loudly from the wall above the doorway. He sighed as he rested his head on his blood stained hands. He glanced over as his wife, Claudia, entered the room. She had been working when Gabriel was brought in. She was still dressed in her nurse scrubs. Victor rose as she walked over and hugged him. "I'm so sorry," she whispered.

Victor looked at her and frowned.

"My brother?" he asked.

"He's in the pediatric ICU right now," Claudia said. "He has massive injuries." Victor nodded slowly. "We don't know if he'll make it," Claudia added. He knew his brother wasn't going anywhere. There was so much more to do.

"Can I see him?" he asked. Claudia put her arm around him as she walked from the room with her husband.

As Victor entered he saw his brother hooked up to machines surrounding the bed. Victor walked around the machines and looked down at his brother. He was badly bruised all over, a white bandage covered his brown hair and tubes went from the machines to his mouth and down his throat. Victor walked over slowly and pulled up a chair. Slowly he took his brother's hand and grasped it as he watched him. Behind him, Jared stood in the corner of the room watching them. "Did the doctor see you?" Victor asked continuing to watch Gabriel but could feel Jared's presence.

"No," Jared said watching Gabriel. Victor sighed. "Are you going to heal all of his injuries?" Jared asked. Victor shook his head.

"I'll give him a few days," he said. "Make it look less miraculous." Jared smiled and shook his head.

"Torture the kid, why don't you?" He mocked.

"What caused the accident?" Victor asked.

"Some man ran the stop light," Jared said.

"Such a shame," Victor said. Jared agreed.

"You would think they would take better care of themselves," he said. "They should be a little less reckless."

"Anything new on this ruler?" he asked.

"No, just waiting in the shadows," Jared said.

Victor nodded as he watched his brother. "Can you leave us for a while?" he asked wanting to be left alone.

"Yes sir," Jared said. "I'll be around if you need me."

Victor glanced over and saw that the room was now empty. He looked back at Gabriel and sighed heavily as he pressed his palm against his brother's forehead. There wasn't time to wait for the healing to begin. It needed to happen quickly.

In a vision, Victor found himself lying on the trail. He sat up and saw that he was no longer wearing a police uniform but wearing black pants and riding boots and white peasant shirt with a solid white shawl over it, a sword hung down on his side. He rose and walked down the trail, he knew exactly where Gabriel would be.

Sunlight lit up the trail as the rays pierced through the tree limbs. He stopped at an opening and saw Gabriel sitting in the grass listening to the waterfall coming down the rocks into a pool of crystal water. He was sitting back with his eyes closed as the sun rained down on him. Victor walked over and squeezed his shoulder. Gabriel looked back at him. "Hello brother," he said.

Victor sat down beside him. "You know, with the end times coming, I could really use your help."

"Oh come on, you can handle it," Gabriel said watching the waterfall. "Much more peaceful here." Victor watched the waterfall and birds and animals roam freely.

"It is," he said with a nod. He looked over at Gabriel as he looked at him.

"Oh come on Victor! I mean, why not let the world deal with their problems?" he asked.

"Because we were assigned to help them," Victor said.

"Well, they kind of messed that all up when Eve ate that fruit," Gabriel said. Victor nodded. Gabriel looked forward then back at him. "It's really messed up," he said. Victor nodded.

"It is," he agreed. Gabriel stared forward then looked over at Victor as Victor remained silent. He nodded and sighed.

"Fine, I'll come back," he said. "Not because it's what you want me to do, but it's what God wants me to do."

"Fine by me," Victor said rising. "I'll see you there, oh, and by the way when you wake up, you're going to be hurting pretty bad just to give you a heads up," Victor said and walked away. Gabriel looked back at the waterfall and sighed.

The next evening Victor sat asleep beside the bed. Gabriel opened his eyes slowly. The tubes had been removed, an oxygen mask remained over his nose and mouth. He looked down at the thick bandage around his arm holding the needles in place then looked over at the machines beeping softly. He could see the sunlight from the sunset piercing through the curtains, giving off a golden glow on the walls. He looked back over at Victor and slowly touched his arm. Victor lifted his head and looked at him. He smiled. "Hey," he said. Gabriel forced a weak smile. "Welcome back to Earth," Victor said. Claudia entered the room and smiled as she walked over to the bed.

"Hey," she said.

"Hi," Gabriel whispered. Claudia smiled as she slowly hugged Victor. Victor smiled as Claudia walked over and checked the machines. She checked Gabriel's pulse and blood pressure and walked from the room. Gabriel groaned as he looked at Victor.

"Told you that you would be hurting," Victor said. Gabriel flinched as he pulled the oxygen mask down.

"Whatever I did to deserve this, Father please forgive me," he whispered. Gabriel cringed and looked up at the ceiling. He looked over at the corner of the room and saw Jared watching. Victor glanced back at Jared.

"Glad to see someone's awake," Jared commented.

"So Damien found his human?" Gabriel asked. Victor nodded.

"It's only a matter of time before he comes to reign," he replied. Gabriel nodded slowly.

"You look good for being in a very bad car wreck," Jared observed, looking at Gabriel.

"Thanks, I don't feel very good," Gabriel responded.

"Welcome to the human world," Jared said. "Enjoy it."

"How can I enjoy when it's so full of hate and people killing each other," Gabriel answered.

"Well, no offense but we did cast Lucifer from Heaven along with some of our brothers and sisters," Victor said.

"That's different! They went against our Father," Gabriel frowned. Victor looked at Jared.

"He's right, they did betray him, and he and his angels betrayed us." Jared responded.

"True, I'm sorry," Victor said.

"You don't have to apologize to me brother," Jared replied. Gabriel cringed.

"What's wrong?" Victor asked.

"I just feel weird," Gabriel said leaning back against the pillow.

"It's called sleep, due to the medication," Jared replied. "They pumped you full of pain medicine." Gabriel groaned.

"You should get some rest, I'll come back later," Victor said as he stood up.

"No!" Gabriel said grabbing his arm. Victor looked down at him. "Don't go," Gabriel said. Jared watched him then looked at Victor. Victor nodded and slowly slid back down into the chair as Gabriel slowly fell into a deep sleep.

While he was asleep, Gabriel remembered back to sitting outside the gates of the Garden of Eden. He was sent to protect the garden from Lucifer or the angels that he might send to destroy it. Sitting back against the pearl wall of the garden, he remembered hearing the animals and the beautiful songs of the birds. It made it very relaxing. There were animals of every kind, trees with different fruit and different herbs. Gabriel glanced back through the gates and stared at the one tree in the center of the garden, but that tree was forbidden. If Adam or Eve ate from it they would be forced from the garden and to never return. Adam knew of this and the punishment that they would endure if they disobeyed. Gabriel turned back and sat back against the wall and listened to the birds chirping.

As time passed Gabriel rose slowly and walked back and forth. Every so often he would catch a glimpse of Eve. She would smile at him but Gabriel would turn away. Adam and Eve were not like him, he had a job to do for his father and he knew the importance of that job.

During one afternoon while Adam was asleep, Eve made her way across a small stream and up to the forbidden fruit tree. She watched the tree and all its beauty. Slowly she ran her hands through the leaves. She looked over as a lizard slowly crawled down a branch.

She smiled as she pulled a piece of fruit from the tree. Holding the fruit in her hand she smiled as she looked back at the lizard. Slowly she took a bite of the fruit and sighed. Gabriel jerked back and stared into the garden. The birds had stopped chirping and the animals became quiet. Eve glanced back at Adam, who was still asleep. She raced back to him and knelt down. He woke and sat up. "What have you done?" he asked seeing the bite that had been taken from the apple.

"It's good," Eve said. "Taste" she said handing him the fruit. Gabriel watched through the gates as Adam ate of the fruit. Quickly, Gabriel raced from the garden's gates.

He raced down the stone walkway and up to the throne. He knelt down and bowed his head. Michael watched him. "Rise," he said. Gabriel rose and made his way up the steps to God. Michael watched Gabriel and looked over at the light on the throne.

"The garden Father, I watched it like you told me to…but something has happened," Gabriel said. "Please! Please Father, do not be angry with me!" Gabriel begged.

"Hold your tongue!" Michael demanded. Gabriel became quiet. Michael turned back to the light. "What should I do Father?" Michael asked gripping the sword on his belt. Gabriel stepped back as the light moved from the chair. Gabriel bowed his head as the light passed him and down to the stone walk way. Michael watched the light disappear. Michael stared at him as Gabriel kept his head lowered.

"Will they die?" he asked.

"I told you to hold your tongue!" Michael demanded. Gabriel became silent as he looked at Michael. His crystal blue eyes held back tears. "Hold your tears, soldier," Michael demanded. Gabriel held back his tears. They glanced down the walk way as God disappeared. Michael stepped in front of Gabriel and walked swiftly down the stone walk way.

They came to the garden and watched God enter. Adam and Eve were nowhere to be seen. "Where art thou?" God called, causing the ground to tremble. Adam and Eve slowly emerged from behind several bushes. They were covered in fig leaves. Gabriel remained silent as Adam and Eve explained how their eyes had been opened to their nakedness. Suddenly the serpent was thrown from the tree by God and turned into a snake. The snake slithered from the garden and disappeared. Michael stepped into the garden and pulled his sword from the sheath on his belt. Flames curled around the sword as he held it pointed at the entrance, which was now the exit of the garden. Adam and Eve sobbed as they slowly walked towards him. Gabriel remained still and silent at the entrance of the garden. They walked from the garden as Michael walked behind them. Gabriel watched God seal the garden and leave. He watched as the beauty now turned to sin and decay. He slowly gripped the bars of the gate as he watched, Michael gripped his shoulder. "Come, my brother," he said. Gabriel slowly walked from the gate behind Michael. He glanced back and saw Lucifer standing at the edge of the garden. The snake slowly curled around his arm as Lucifer smiled at him.

Gabriel jerked awake in the hospital bed with a scream and sat up frantically. He looked for his dagger as he sobbed. Victor woke with a jerk. "Hey! Hey!" Victor said.

"He's here! He's here! I saw him!" Gabriel screamed. Victor grabbed his arms.

"Hey! Look at me!" he demanded. Gabriel looked at him. "There's no one here," Victor said. Gabriel looked around the room. It was true, they were the only ones there, there had been no visitors from school or from their church, they had all been by earlier.

"The garden," Gabriel whispered looking back at him. "The tree!" Victor fell silent.

"It wasn't your fault," he said.

"I was given a job, I failed!" Gabriel replied.

"None of my soldiers…my brothers, have ever failed," Victor said.

"Lucifer did," Gabriel frowned.

"He turned his back on us," Victor said. "He's no longer our brother but our enemy and when he rises I will strike him down. Besides, when this war takes place, I trust no one at my side but my brother Gabriel, my second in command," he said. Gabriel nodded. Victor smiled. "You know, I love you," he said. Gabriel nodded. Victor gently pulled him into a hug. Gabriel hugged him tightly. He felt the calming sense that only Michael could provide. He always looked after his soldiers and was the commander in chief when it came to God's army. Gabriel slowly laid back on the bed and watched Victor. Jared sat silently in the chair across the room watching. Victor slowly pressed his palm against Gabriel's forehead and shut his eyes. Gabriel slowly slipped into a deep, silent sleep. Victor looked at him and sighed as he slowly rose.

"People are going ask questions if his wounds heal all at once," Jared said. Victor walked over to the window and looked out.

"He was hurting," he said.

"I'm just saying," Jared began.

"Well, don't!" Victor snapped, looking at him. Jared sat back in the chair. Victor shook his head as he looked back out the window. When he turned and looked back at the chair, he saw that it was empty.

Claudia entered. "Hey," he said, walking over to her.

"Came to give him some more pain medicine," Claudia smiled.

"I wouldn't bother him, he's sleeping," Victor said.

"But he needs something for the pain," Claudia said.

"Don't worry, I'll let you know when he wakes up," Victor said. Claudia nodded slowly.

"How are you doing?" she asked. Victor shrugged.

"I'm okay," he said.

"Any plans for the funerals yet?" Claudia asked. Victor shook his head.

"I don't do funerals," he replied. Claudia nodded slowly as she rubbed his arm. They stood looking out the window.

"The city is so beautiful at night," Claudia said as she hugged Victor slowly. Lights flickered in the sky. "Oh wow! The northern lights!" Claudia said with a smile. Victor stared at the sky as flashes of green, pink and purple moved across like curtains. Gabriel opened his eyes and looked over at the window. Victor watched silently. Slowly the lights faded and once again the sky turned dark. Victor turned back and watched Gabriel fall back into a deep sleep. "You know I never heard about your real parents," Claudia said. Victor remained silent not quite sure what to tell her. God was his father and that's all he would ever tell anyone.

"Maybe another time," Victor said. Claudia nodded.

"Okay," she said. "Remember we have the church event on Sunday."

"You know I wouldn't miss it," Victor grinned. Claudia smiled and kissed his cheek as she walked from the room. Victor smiled and looked back out the window.

CHAPTER TWO

A few days later Victor pushed Gabriel down the sidewalk in the wheel chair. "You excited to be out of the hospital?" Victor asked. After being commanded to hold his tongue for so long by Michael, he finally felt free to speak.

"You have no idea," Gabriel said. Victor smiled as he pushed the wheelchair over to Claudia's car.

"Claudia's going to take you to the house. I have to get to work," Victor said. Gabriel nodded as Victor knelt down beside the chair. "I should be home about ten tonight," Victor said. "You can go back to school when you're ready," he said squeezing his brother's shoulders. Claudia walked from the building with a smile.

"Are you ready to get home?" she asked. Gabriel smiled and nodded.

"More than you know," he said. He helped rise with Victor's help and sat down in the passenger seat of the car. Claudia slowly kissed Victor's cheek and smiled.

"See you tonight," she said. Victor nodded and pushed the wheelchair back into the hospital.

Claudia stared forward as she drove down the highway towards their neighborhood. "I know you probably miss your parents," she said. Gabriel looked over at her.

"Yeah," he said looking back out the window. Gabriel stared at a billboard sign ahead, it read "*God's truth are fairy tales.*" Gabriel looked over at Claudia. "When did they start putting those signs up?" he asked.

"That one went up last week," Claudia said. "Such hateful messages, it makes me sick." Gabriel agreed, the messages seemed to be coming up everywhere, no one seemed to understand what was going on, and nor did they seem to care. "I'm sure they'll be happy to have you back at school," Claudia said. Gabriel nodded, not really wanting to go back. He couldn't help but over hear stories from kids in the lunch room about sex and drugs.

"I don't understand people," Gabriel whispered.

"Why's that?" Claudia asked.

"I don't understand how they can hate God so much," Gabriel said.

"You and me both," Claudia said with a nod. She looked back forward as they continued home.

That night Claudia was lying next to Victor awake. "I hope he likes it here," she said. Victor looked at her and smiled.

"Oh, I'm sure he will," he said. "Who wouldn't love a massive room and a huge pool in the backyard."

"I'm going to go check on him once more before we go to sleep." Victor nodded as Claudia rose and walked from the room.

Claudia entered the room and stopped, seeing Gabriel sitting on the side of his bed watching the window. "Sweetheart, you okay?" she asked entering the room. Gabriel continued to watch the window silently as if he was in a trance. Claudia walked over and sat down beside him. "You should be resting," she said.

"I'm not tired," Gabriel whispered continuing to stare at the window. Claudia looked over at the window and saw the moon slowly appear from behind the clouds.

"What are you watching?" she asked.

"The night sky, the way God meant for it to be," Gabriel said. Claudia looked at the window. The clouds had cleared and the stars sparkled brightly.

"You should be resting," Claudia repeated.

"No," Gabriel whispered staring ahead. "I miss it."

"Miss what?" Claudia asked.

"I miss the beautiful blue skies, the green grass and trees," Gabriel said.

"Honey, it is fall, all that will return in spring," Claudia said. Gabriel looked at her slowly.

"There won't be a spring," he said. "He's coming."

Claudia grinned. "Sweetie, what are you talking about?" she asked. Gabriel looked back at the window.

"He'll come like a thief in the night," he whispered.

"Honey, this must be a side effect from the pain medicine," Claudia said. Gabriel continued to stare forward. Claudia gently combed his hair from his face. She felt his forehead. "You're burning up," she said.

"I'm fine," Gabriel said looking at her.

"Lay down," Claudia said.

"No! You have to understand what I say," Gabriel said.

"I understand, the rapture will happen, and I know it will," Claudia said.

"The days will get worse," Gabriel said. Claudia stared down at him. "It is seen in the prophecy," Gabriel said. "...as it was foretold by John!" Claudia sighed as she shook her head.

"Honey, please, lay down," she said as Victor entered the room.

"Tell her!" Gabriel said, looking at Victor.

"He's burning up," Claudia frowned. Gabriel rose and walked over to Victor.

"Tell her about the prophecy!" he begged. Victor took his arms and pulled him over to the bed.

"She's right, you're burning up," he said forcing him to sit down.

"You have to tell her! She needs to know!" Gabriel continued to beg.

Victor nodded. "I'll tell her," he said.

"I'll get the thermometer," Claudia said, racing from the room. Victor forced Gabriel to lie back on the bed. He pulled the covers up over him. Gabriel turned his head from side to side. Claudia returned with the thermometer and handed it to Victor. Victor pressed the thermometer against Gabriel's ear.

"They need to know," Gabriel said.

"I'll make sure I tell them," Victor said. The thermometer beeped. Victor took it and read it. "One hundred and four," he said. Claudia cringed.

"Let me get some fever reducer," she said. Claudia raced from the room. Victor looked down at Gabriel.

"They're talking, I can hear them," Gabriel whispered as he shook his head.

"I know! I can hear them too," Victor said.

"You have to tell her about you," Gabriel said. Victor shook his head.

"She's human, she won't understand," he said. Claudia stood at the door.

"Won't understand what?" she asked walking up to the bed.

"It's nothing," Victor said taking the medicine bottle.

"Victor, what is going on?" Claudia asked.

"It's complicated!" Victor said pouring some medicine into a small cup and lifting Gabriel's head to it. Gabriel drank it down and rested his head back down on the pillow. Claudia handed Victor a washcloth. He slowly pressed it down over his brother's forehead.

"You can talk to me," Claudia said.

"It's not something you should be involved in," Victor said.

"Why not?" Claudia asked.

"Because...because I don't want you to be involved in it," Victor said.

"We're married, we should be able to talk to each other about things," Claudia said walking from the room. Victor sighed and looked down at his brother. He slowly rose from the bed and followed Claudia from the room.

He entered the main bedroom behind her. "I can't make you understand what is going on," he said. Claudia turned back to him.

"You haven't tried to explain it to me," she snapped. Victor sighed as looked down at her. "Please, please, Victor, what is going on?"

"I'm not who you think I am," Victor said not wanting to have to go into deep details. Claudia frowned. "So...who are you?" Claudia asked.

"My brother and I are different from people here," Victor said.

"Let me guess, you're aliens?" Claudia said with a smile. Victor forced a smile.

"Something, like that," he whispered. Claudia's smile faded.

"Victor, what is going on? Just tell me," she said. Victor slowly pulled his shirt off. Claudia rose, seeing healed scars covering his back. "What happened?" she asked slowly touching them.

"I was in a war," Victor said. Claudia lowered her hand.

"I didn't know you were in the military," Claudia said.

"Not the military here," Victor said looking back at her.

"Please say you're not a terrorist," Claudia said. "Or I'll have to walk out that door right now."

"I'm not a terrorist and neither is my brother," Victor said. "I went to war against my brother," he said.

"Against Gabriel?" Claudia asked.

"No, my other brother," Victor said.

"I didn't know you had any other brothers," Claudia said.

"My Father banished him," Victor said. "Along with those that followed him." Claudia slowly sat down on the bed. "We were sent to protect people from them. But that plan had failed and now he's coming back with an army." Claudia grinned and looked at him.

"What is your family the mafia or something?" she asked. Victor smiled and walked over to the window.

"No, my Father created this world," he said. "There is a prophecy that Christ will return and until that time the anti-Christ will take his stand."

"That's in the Bible you know," Claudia said. Victor nodded.

"I know," he said. "It was written by witnesses and by those given the gift from my Father. That time is coming, the prophecy will be fulfilled."

"Where do you stand in all this? What makes you different?" Claudia asked. Victor turned back to her.

"I was sent here to find my brother and put an end to his reign," he said.

"I'm not following," Claudia said. Victor sighed as he took her hands.

"I'm not from here," he said. Claudia stared at him. "The war lasted for years," Victor began as he remembered back to the war.

Michael, Gabriel and thousands of angels marched unto the battlefield. They stopped as they saw Lucifer and his angels waiting. Lucifer watched him and smiled. "Hello, brother!" he called. Michael gripped the sword on his belt as he watched his brother. The angels behind Lucifer cheered as Lucifer mocked Michael, by pretending to grab his sword and walk around with his chest pushed out. Gabriel looked over at Michael then back at Lucifer. Michael pulled the sword from his belt. "You think you frighten me?" Lucifer shouted pulling a sword from his belt. Michael lifted his sword to the sky as lightening flashed striking the sword. Flames rippled down the blade, setting the metal glowing red and flames shooting out from blade. Lucifer's smile faded as he stared at Michael. The angels behind Michael stood firm as they waited for the order. The land of Megiddo was empty and at the time only a desert. Lucifer smiled and bowed to him. "Go ahead, send me your best warriors, I will rip out their throats and feed them to my men," Lucifer called. Gabriel gripped his sword as he watched ahead at the army in front of them. Michael looked back at his angels then at Lucifer.

"I will not take it easy on you, brother!" he called.

"I wouldn't expect you to," Lucifer called. "You're just as weak as your army. Go ahead brother! Send them to me." Lucifer's army stood behind him silently. They slowly looked at one another nervously then they looked back at the army before them. Lucifer held out his hand in front of him sending a wall of fire to rise between him and Michael's army.

"Is that all you have brother?" Michael called. He lifted his sword as lightening flashed striking the ground behind Lucifer's army and sending a wall of fire surrounding them.

Lucifer glared back angrily at Michael. "Go ahead! Give me what you got!" he shouted. The fire raged violently. The smoke and heat was intense as Michael and his army moved forward. Lucifer looked over at his army. "Take no prisoners!" he shouted. "Kill them all!" Michael lifted up his sword as the angels charged behind him. The ground rumbled loudly as lightning struck all around them causing more flames to rise and more smoke to fill the sky. Michael charged through the flames taking no heed to the pain for they could feel nothing. The army of angels followed him with their weapons in their hands. The ground shook violently as the angels clashed. Michael raced to Lucifer and slid across the ground, ducking beneath Lucifer's sword as he swung at him. Michael rose and turned back as Lucifer swung at him. The sky lit up with lightning and the roll of thunder could be heard all around. Lucifer smiled as he kicked Michael back. He turned back as Gabriel appeared close by. Michael looked over at him.

"No!" he shouted rising and racing towards them. Lucifer walked towards Gabriel with his sword in hand.

"Gabriel, always my favorite brother. So young! So handsome!" Lucifer said slowly circling him as the other fallen angels held Michael back. Michael watched Gabriel. "You know, your brother always hated you," Lucifer said looking over at Michael and smiling. "He blamed you for letting me enter the garden." Gabriel stared at Michael. Michael struggled against the angels holding him back. "Drop your sword and join me, we can take control of the Earth and they will bow before me," he said. Gabriel continued to stare forward at Michael. Michael shook his head as fear and heartbreak filled his eyes. Lucifer leaned in and whispered in Gabriel's ear. "Your Father no longer loves you. I do! Come, join my army and help us rejoice in this kingdom," he said with a hiss. He slowly slid his fingers across the back of Gabriel's neck. "So…what do you say, brother?" Lucifer said wrapping his arm around Gabriel's shoulders. Michael struggled hard against the fallen angels. Lucifer smiled as he stared at Michael. Gabriel looked at Lucifer.

"Brother….you know me too well," he said. "You know as much as I loved my brothers I could never abandon them." Lucifer laughed loudly and clapped.

"Then you will join us!" Lucifer called. The angels cheered loudly. Michael stared at Gabriel in shock then turned his head in shame. Gabriel watched as Michael frowned. Turning back to Lucifer, Gabriel slowly pulled a dagger from his pocket. Michael turned back to the sound of the blade leaving the sheath. Lucifer stopped. "You think that wise boy?" he said turning back as several fallen angels grabbed Gabriel's arms and forced him to the ground. The dagger landed in the dirt. "You would stab your own brother in the back?" Lucifer shouted. The fallen angels held back Michael and his men. Lucifer yanked Gabriel to his feet by his hair. "You know what they do to soldiers that abandon their own army?" he called as he dragged Gabriel to the view of his own army. "They are judged and sentenced to death." Gabriel screamed as Lucifer yanked his arms back. Lucifer shoved Gabriel to his knees. "Here is your reward boys!" Lucifer called. Gabriel looked at Michael. Michael broke free from their grasp and raced over to his brother. He pulled Gabriel over to him as Lucifer smiled. "Aw, how sweet!" Lucifer hissed as he stepped back with his army. Michael stood as his men gathered behind him. Gabriel watched as the smoke and flames cleared and Lucifer and his men disappeared.

Claudia sat back on the bed as Victor finished the story. "So…you mean to tell me…this war you fought in was against the devil?" she asked in disbelief. Victor stood at the window watching outside.

"Correct term is Lucifer," he said. "But after the war he was known by the angels as Satan or to humans as the devil." Claudia smiled as she shook her head. Victor looked back at her.

"So you mean to tell me that kid in the other room carried around a sword and a dagger?" she asked rising.

"He's a warrior not a kid," Victor said.

"He's seventeen years old!" Claudia said. "He's a kid. And how would you explain the no talking or anything like that?"

"He didn't trust humans," Victor said. Claudia laughed and shook her head.

"So you fought an angel with horns and a tail?" she asked.

"Technically that's not correct, Lucifer was a handsome angel, not every picture you look at is going to show you who he truly was," Victor said. Claudia shook her head.

"This is getting too strange for me. I think you've been working on the police force too long," she said starting for the door.

"Look, please, just…just, hear me out," Victor said. Claudia sighed and looked back at him, not sure if she could take much more.

Gabriel laid asleep in bed as rain slowly drained down the window like snakes. He woke as lightening flashed outside. Sitting up, he watched the window as tree limbs scratched at the screen like long claws. Gabriel turned and pulled the dagger from the drawer of his desk. Behind him a shadow moved against the wall and hid in the darkness in the corner. Gabriel glanced back as everything became still. He continued to sit in bed as he watched the room, scouting for movement in the darkness. Lightening flashed outside as Gabriel looked away from the corner. A man stood in the corner of the room watching him. As he glanced back, darkness consumed the room again. He sighed and laid back down in the bed. He slid the dagger beneath the pillow feeling someone watching him from behind. The figure moved past the shadow towards the bed. He slowly slid his hand across the covers at Gabriel's throat. Gabriel stared forward feeling the movement behind him. He felt the long nails as it slid across his throat. "No!" he screamed jerking back. He aimed the dagger out into the darkness. Victor raced into the room with his gun drawn. Gabriel breathed heavily as he clutched the dagger tightly.

Victor lowered the gun as he walked over to the bed. Gabriel looked around the room and looked back at Victor. Victor slowly took Gabriel by the wrist and lowered the dagger. He slid it from Gabriel's hand and placed it back in the drawer as Claudia came to the door. "There was someone here," Gabriel whispered.

"There's not now," Victor said sitting beside him. Victor laid the gun on the dresser. "Lightening can make you see things," he said.

"He was here," Gabriel gasped. "He was going for my neck." Victor felt his forehead, he was still burning up. Gabriel groaned. He slowly laid back down as Victor took his temperature. The thermometer beeped softly as Victor looked down at it.

"One hundred and five," he said, looking over at Claudia.

"It has to be an infection somewhere. Probably from the wreck," Claudia said. "I'll give the doctor a call," she said.

"Why must we suffer for their mistakes?" Gabriel asked, staring at his brother. Claudia stopped and stared back into the room. "I mean Eve ate the fruit, she knew…she knew what would happen," Gabriel said. Victor held the wash cloth against Gabriel's forehead as he watched him. "Adam didn't try and stop her. I never understood why," Gabriel whispered.

"Don't talk," Victor said knowing the aggravation was making it worse. His skin was becoming more and more pale. Victor looked over at Claudia then back down at Gabriel.

"Our Father…he was so angry," Gabriel whispered, bearly having enough strength to speak.

"Gabe stop talking, you're draining your strength," Victor said pressing the wash cloth against his cheek.

"I'm calling an ambulance!" Claudia said as she started for the door.

"They won't make it in time," Victor said seeing Gabriel's condition worsening. He could heal him but he knew that Claudia would ask questions. Claudia looked back at him as Victor looked at her. Claudia shook her head.

"I thought…you told her," Gabriel whispered.

Victor forced a faint smile and nodded. "I did," he said. Claudia walked over and knelt down beside the bed. She fought back tears as she stared at Gabriel. Gabriel struggled to force out words as Victor slowly pressed his palm against Gabriel's forehead and shut his eyes, knowing there was no option left. Tears stream down Claudia's face as she rested her head down on the bed.

Early the next morning Claudia woke from her sleep and sat back from the bed. She watched as Gabriel laid motionless on the bed. She sobbed as she moved from the bed. She had seen dying before and she knew that it had happened over night. She stopped, seeing Victor standing at the window looking outside. The morning was still dark. "I'm so sorry," she whispered. Victor glanced back at her.

"His fever broke," Victor said.

"What?" Claudia asked. "When?"

"About one this morning," Victor said.

"But his fever was one hundred and five," Claudia said. "He could barely breathe!" She looked down at Gabriel as he slowly turned on his side still asleep. She gently felt his forehead. His skin was now cool. "But…but how?" she asked. "He was dying." Victor remained silent. Claudia frowned and shook her head. "So this goes back to how you and he are angels," she said shaking her head. "What? Did you heal him?" she asked. Victor watched her silently. Claudia turned and walked away.

"I can't make you understand," he said. Claudia looked back at him.

"You're my husband! Make me understand!" she shouted. Gabriel woke and looked back at her as he sat up in bed. He looked back over at Victor. Victor shook his head. "I can't," he said.

"I knew it," she said. She stormed from the room. Gabriel looked over at Victor as he glanced back out the window.

"You're a great warrior, you know," he said.

"Not here though," he whispered. "I'm human here!"

"Our father gave you a great gift," Gabriel said rising from the bed. "To make people understand! To make people see…show her, you're losing her." He watched as Victor walked from the room quickly.

He entered his bedroom and watched Claudia slowly pack her suit case. "I can't take this Victor!" she yelled angrily.

"Let me show you," Victor said.

"Show me what…your wings…your halo?" she asked.

Victor smiled and shook his head. "We don't have halos," he said.

"Great, you're mocking me," Claudia said. Victor walked over to her and took her hand. She pulled her hand away and continued to pack.

"Let me show you my home," Victor said. Claudia stared at him. Victor slowly took her hands and guided her away from the bed. Claudia shook her head. "I have to go," she said pulling away.

"Please! Give me a chance," Victor said. Claudia sighed and stared at Victor.

"You can't stop me from leaving," she frowned. "I've made up my mind."

"I understand," Victor said walking over to her. Slowly he took her hands. She looked into his eyes and shook her head.

"Deep down inside I hoped…I hoped that you were different," she said, "but you're just like us…you're human." She walked away from him. Slowly Victor took his shirt off and shut the curtains. Claudia turned back. "Victor…" she began but stopped as the lights flickered.

"My name is Michael," he said. Claudia shook her head as she shut the suitcase and pulled it from the bed. The light bulb blew out beside the bed. Claudia turned back as Victor stared at her. Slowly wings emerged from his back. Claudia gasped in shock as she backed away. The wings slowly spread across the room. Claudia gasped as she stared at Victor. She slowly stepped forward holding out her hand. Victor slowly took her hand. She slid her other hand down his cheek. Going into kiss him, she pulled back as he turned his head. "I can't," Victor whispered. He looked back down at her as the wings slowly fade.

"But, I'm your wife," Claudia whispered.

"You're Victor's wife," he said. "I can't give you what you seek."

"Why?" Claudia asked. "This is what you wanted me to see!"

"Before the morning sun rises you will not be here," Victor said.

"What?" Claudia asked.

"The kingdom awaits," Victor said, kissing her cheek. Claudia watched him walk from the room.

She walked over to the window and looked up as she opened the curtains. The clouds slowly began to part as the sun slowly rose in the distance. She smiled, as the sound of a trumpet could be heard.

CHAPTER THREE

Gabriel lay asleep on the bed as the sun slowly came through the windows. He jerked awake and sat up. He glanced over at the window and shoved the covers back as he rose up. He walked over to the window and looked out. The sounds of screams and the ground rumbling could be heard. He quickly raced from the room. "Victor!" he shouted. Victor raced upstairs with two duffle bags.

"Get packed!" he called, handing one bag to Gabriel. Gabriel followed Victor into the empty room. Victor pressed his palm against the wall. The walls begin to slowly slide apart revealing weapons, such as swords, bow and arrows and daggers.

"Victor…. it's happened, hasn't it?" Gabriel asked.

"Go, get your stuff together!" Victor commanded. Gabriel raced from the room. Victor quickly began to pile weapons into the duffle bags. Jared entered the room. He quickly grabbed weapons from the wall and shoved them into his bags as well.

"We have to get going," he said. The house shook violently as a plane crashed several blocks away. Victor and Jared grabbed the bags and swung them over their shoulders. "Let's go!" Jared called, racing from the room. Victor quickly followed as Gabriel raced from the room with several bags of clothes. They hurried down the steps and outside as people ran frantically from their homes. Chaos had begun to take over the neighborhood. People were now in a state of panic seeing their children's clothes lying on the floor but finding them nowhere. Clothes also laid in the streets, from where joggers and other pedestrians had suddenly vanished.

They quickly climbed into their car. Victor put the car in drive and sped from the driveway and quickly headed down the street. Driverless cars were blocking their lane. Victor swerved to miss the cars as he sped through the neighborhood. Gabriel gasped as a plane crashed into the city causing a large explosion and debris to fall in every direction. "We have to get out of this area!" Jared called.

"I know!" Victor called back, speeding unto the highway. He slammed on the brakes and groaned, seeing traffic at a complete stand still. There were empty cars in every direction. Gabriel stared forward. "Stay here," Victor said as he got out of the car.

"Where are you going?" Gabriel called. Jared watched as several people raced over to Victor, begging for help as they saw his police uniform. There was a thunderous roar as Jared and Gabriel glanced back. A driverless eighteen-wheeler was coming through the traffic shoving cars violently from the road. Jared quickly got out of the car.

"Come on!" he shouted. Gabriel quickly climbed from the seat towards the open the door. He jerked back as the eighteen-wheeler slammed into a car and rolled on to its side, crushing cars beneath it. It slid violently across the road, slamming into the police cruiser and sending it flipping violently into the ditch. Jared sat up slowly from the grass close by and looked over at the car. Victor struggled to get away from the crowd gathered around him. Jared raced over to the car and knelt down.

Gabriel gasped and woke as Jared reached in for him. "Come on!" Jared shouted reaching through the shattered window. Gabriel quickly slid over to him. Jared pulled him from the vehicle. They turned back and grabbed the gear from the crushed car. Victor broke away from the people as they continued to scream for help and ask him what had just happened.

He raced over to Gabriel and Jared ignoring their pleas.

"You guys alright?" he asked. Gabriel nodded as he twisted his arm and the bone snapped back together. He sighed as he rubbed his arm as it healed.

"Yeah! We're good," he said with a nod. Victor grabbed the duffle bags, as Jared and Gabriel grabbed one each. They quickly raced down the highway, avoiding people and questions about what was happening. They came to the end of the highway and stopped. They glanced back and saw the city in the distance. Many buildings were on fire and screams and cries could be heard coming from all around by those left behind. Victor shook his head and turned away. Jared and Gabriel quickly followed.

In a small neighborhood, Jared led the way towards a small town house. Victor and Gabriel followed. "Are you sure she's here?" Victor asked.

"Positive!" Jared said walking up the brick steps and ringing the doorbell. There was no answer. He rang the doorbell again and waited.

"I don't think she's here," Gabriel said. Jared looked back at him then back at the door. He forced the door open with a push. They quickly entered, shutting and locking the door behind them.

Gabriel lowered the bag as he glanced around. He walked over to the hall and saw photographs of the family who once lived there. But one person was missing from each of them and that was Anastasia. She had been adopted just like them. It was the only way for them to fit in with a family. Victor walked into the living room and sat the bag down on the couch. He sat down and sighed as he glanced around the living room. He smiled seeing angel figures on the fireplace mantel. Slowly he picked up a Bible from the table in front of the couch. Gabriel walked over and sat down beside him as Victor looked through the Bible. Victor stopped at the picture of the Garden of Eden. A man and woman shared fruit in the picture. Gabriel sighed as he looked away. "We have to keep moving," Victor said shutting the Bible and laying it back down. "I'm going to see if there's a car we can use," he said rising and walking from the room. Gabriel stared down at the Bible as Victor walked outside.

Victor spotted a car across the street. He walked over to it and pulled out a paperclip from his shirt pocket as he walked to the trunk of the car. He forced the paperclip into the lock and turned it. It popped loudly and lifted. Victor cleared the everyday items, like a spare tire, and items for the engine, from the trunk and laid them on the side of the road. He sighed seeing plenty of room for the bags. He stopped feeling someone watching him. He closed the trunk and drew his gun. He lowered it seeing Anastasia sitting Indian style on the top of the car. Her long brown hair was in a braid, and she still wore her blue jeans and white tank top covered by a jean vest. He placed the gun back on his belt as Anastasia slid down from the car. "If it isn't Michael himself," she said walking over to the trunk of the car. Victor looked over at her.

"Where have you been?" Victor asked continuing to clear the trunk.

"Just viewing the situation," Anastasia replied. Jared and Gabriel walked outside. Anastasia glanced back and smiled. Jared smiled and walked over and hugged her. Anastasia looked over at Gabriel and smiled. "It's good to see you," she said. Gabriel smiled and nodded.

"You too," he grinned. Anastasia looked back at Victor.

"It's dangerous taking a car, they have road blocks," she warned. Victor looked at her.

"Already?" he asked. Anastasia nodded.

"Apparently they think the Christians are responsible for the chaos," she said. "They see this many weapons in a car and they'll think you're up to something." Victor groaned. "They set up camps in every state,"

"Camps?" Gabriel said.

Anastasia looked over at him. "For the new Christians. Some that were thinking about being saved before the rapture, and now that the rapture has happened they are Christians. The officers will go through each town and whatever Christian they find they'll be placed in the labor camps, forced to take the mark of the beast and if they don't….they'll be killed." Victor sighed heavily as he looked down at the trunk.

"We have to take the car, if we don't, we have no way of traveling. We have to get to the Middle East," he said. "We'll have to take the back roads to get to the dock. Get packed, we'll be heading out in the morning," he said, shutting the trunk of the car.

As night came Anastasia quickly filled several bags with cans of food from the kitchen cabinets. Jared handed her a Bible. She placed it in the bag and placed several bags and cans of food over it. Slowly she pulled her cross necklace from her pocket and stared at it. Jared looked down at it and sighed. She unhooked it and placed it around her neck. "Be not ashamed," she said looking over at Jared. Jared nodded as they zipped up the bag. Gabriel hurried into the room.

"Come here," he called. They quickly hurried into the living room. Jared and Anastasia entered the living room to find Victor watching the television.

The news was on every channel, and the reporter was speaking with Mason. "So what do you think happen to over millions and millions of people?" the reporter asked.

"I believe that this is somehow connected to Christians," Mason answered. "They were a threat to our society and now we see how that affected everyone."

Anastasia slowly sat down on the couch and listened. "How do you plan to help those that were affected by this chaos?" the reporter asked.

"By enforcing change, those that were left behind are to turn in any Christian that is spotted wearing a cross or carrying a Bible," Mason said. Anastasia continued to sit quietly. Gabriel looked over at Victor and sighed heavily.

"Are you sure taking a car will be such a great idea?" Jared asked looking at Victor.

"We have no other option at this point," Victor said. "We'll rest here for the night, and take off before the sun rises, maybe the guards won't be as alert." The others nodded.

"We'll take the rooms upstairs," Jared said rising.

"We'll sleep down here," Victor said. Gabriel nodded.

As night came, Gabriel sat on the floor beside the couch. Victor slowly turned a blade between his fingers as Gabriel watched him. Victor looked over at him and saw Gabriel struggling to keep his eyes open. "You need to get some sleep," he said.

"I'm not tired," Gabriel said. He yawned and sat back. Victor shook his head seeing that his brother was exhausted.

"Yeah, you don't seem tired," he said. Gabriel glared at him. "Bundle up on that couch and sleep," Victor said.

"What if someone comes by?" Gabriel asked.

"I'll keep an eye out," Victor replied. Gabriel nodded and slowly rose. He laid down on the couch and fell asleep facing the back of the couch. Victor sat back against the wall listening for any sounds of approaching vehicles. Slowly he drifted off into a deep sleep.

After an hour, Victor woke to the sound of trucks. He glanced over and saw lights reflecting through the windows. He ducked down as the lights came through. Glancing back he watched Gabriel remain still. "Don't move," he whispered knowing that one movement the light would pick up on it. The light moved off Gabriel as he stirred slowly in his sleep. Victor quickly crawled over to him "Gabriel!" he called shaking him. The sound of another truck could be heard coming. He could see the light coming down the road as the truck got closer. "Gabriel!" he shouted shaking him harder.

"What?" Gabriel asked looking back at him. He saw the light getting closer. He quickly slid from the couch and crawled with Victor over to the wall. They sat quietly and listened as the truck passed by. "Who are they?" he whispered.

"Guards," Victor whispered. He listened to the sound of men talking outside. He jumped hearing one of the men kick open a door to a house across the street. They could hear screaming from a man and woman as they were dragged from the house to the truck. More lights could be seen coming down the road. They slid away from the window and over to the corner and listened as the guards talked close by.

"Search every house," one of the guards said as they moved away from the home. Victor listened as the movement become quieter. He sighed as he slowly moved away from the window. Suddenly the door was kicked in as guards moved in with guns drawn. Victor held up his hands as the guards aimed the guns at him and Gabriel.

"Take them to the truck," the lead guard said.

Victor and Gabriel were led outside with their hands behind their heads. Victor glanced over as Anastasia and Jared watched from the woods close by. They managed to get away unseen or detected by the guards. Victor motioned for them to go with a nod of his head. Jared and Anastasia disappeared into the woods. Victor glanced back forward as the guard walked over to him and knocked him out with the butt of the gun.

Victor woke to the feeling of the truck moving. He groaned and touched his forehead. He gasped seeing bodies piled into the back of the bed of the truck. He jerked up quickly and stopped seeing Gabriel sitting beside him. "Are you alright?" Victor asked. Gabriel nodded as Victor pulled him close, he could see the fear in Gabriel's eyes as he watched the humans around them.

"How old is the boy?" A man asked from the darkness. Victor glanced back and saw at least twenty people packed together tightly in the truck.

"Seventeen," Victor said continuing to hug Gabriel tightly. He could feel the tension of the people around him.

"Is he your son?" one man asked.

"No, he's my brother," Victor said. The man smiled.

"So young and innocent, I like that," the man said. "Why don't you let him come and sit with me?"

"You hurt my brother in anyway, you'll be joining these bodies there," Victor snapped. The man laughed and sat back against the wall of the truck.

"Tell me kid, what is your name?" the man asked.

"Don't speak to anybody," Victor whispered. Gabriel remained silent as he sat close to Victor.

"Oh come on! I'm not going to hurt the kid," the man said. Gabriel remained quiet as he watched the men along the wall of the truck stare at him. He was the youngest of the people in the truck. Many of them stared at him as if he was a piece of meat. This didn't sit well with Victor. Victor continued to block him from the view of the men. The men looked away from them becoming somewhat annoyed.

Victor sat quietly against the wall of the truck. It bounced along the road but it was so dark he couldn't see anything. The brisk cool air made it impossible to stay warm in the truck, even though there were so many people packed together. Gabriel rubbed his arms, trying to warm up. Victor wrapped his arm around him and pulled him close. Gabriel leaned against him.

"I want to go back," he whispered. "I hate it here."

"Me too," Victor whispered. Gabriel shivered, he hated the cold. That was one thing he could not get use to on Earth. A man across from them slowly handed Victor a green blanket. Victor took it and nodded. "Thank you," he whispered. The man smiled. Gabriel sat forward slowly as Victor placed it around him. He leaned back against Victor. Victor watched the man. "Why are you here?" he asked.

"They caught me stealing," the man named, Kyle said. "It was a bad move on my part," he said.

"Stealing what?" Victor asked.

"Bibles," Kyle answered.

"Why steal Bibles?" Victor asked.

"Because there were no owners at the store and I wanted to hand them out," he replied.

"You're a Christian?" Victor asked.

"I thought I was," Kyle said. "I mean my wife and I said the prayer to accept Christ, but apparently it wasn't the right prayer. We worked so hard to do well, and be good Christian people. Somehow God forgot about us."

Victor shook his head. "He didn't forget," he said. "God hears every prayer. Don't worry, God hears everything." Kyle nodded. Victor rested his head against the boards behind him. He watched the men close by watching Gabriel. Their intentions were beyond evil, and Victor wasn't about to let the men get close to his brother. Victor looked back as lights could be seen. "Where are we going?" he asked.

"To one of the thousands of camps positioned in every state," Kyle said.

"What is it for?" Victor asked.

"For Christians, along with the criminally insane," Kyle said looking at the men beside him. One of the men smiled and looked at Victor and Gabriel. Victor looked over at two elderly men sitting side by side. He had met them before, but not on Earth. He smiled and looked back forward.

"How are you guys holding up?" Victor asked. The men looked over at him, one spoke in Hebrew. Victor smiled. "I understand," he said.

"What did he say?" Kyle asked.

"He said it'll be over soon," Victor replied. Kyle nodded slowly. The truck began to slow down as it turned. Gabriel sat forward and looked back through the small space between the boards of the truck and the canopy over them. He could see thick, jail like fences surrounding the camp and hundreds of long buildings side by side. He could see groups of people being led from the buildings and to a large stone building with smoke coming from a large chimney like structure. He quickly turned away and leaned back against Victor. "We have nothing to fear!" Victor whispered, pulling him close.

"We have everything to fear," Gabriel whispered. "It's a torture compound meant to hurt people."

"It'll be alright," Victor whispered. He was interrupted by the sound of gates opening. Guards could be heard calling orders out to the driver. The truck pulled to a stop and the back door opened.

"All women to the right, all men to the left. Do we have any young kids or teenagers?" the guard called shining his flashlight into the truck.

"One," the driver said. The driver shown his light on Gabriel.

"Leave him in the truck," the guard called. Gabriel watched as the people were being led from the truck. Victor remained beside Gabriel. "Let's go!" the guard called.

"I'm not leaving my brother!" Victor called. Several guards climbed into the truck and dragged Victor away from Gabriel. "No!" Victor shouted as he was dragged away from Gabriel. Several guards stepped into the truck and handcuffed Gabriel's hands to the floor bed. Gabriel stared at Victor in fear.

"We have no more room for another teenager," the guard called.

Victor looked back at the guard. "Then put him in a cell with me!" he called. The guard punched him and knocked him to the ground.

"I give orders here!" the guard called. Gabriel pulled on the handcuffs. He watched them pull Victor away from the truck. "No! No! Victor!" he screamed pulling on the shackles. "Victor, don't leave me!" he screamed. Victor fought against the guards as they dragged him further away from the truck.

"Burn the truck, get rid of the bodies," one guard called.

"No! No!" Victor screamed as they dragged him into one of the buildings.

The smell was awful as Victor continued to struggle against the guards. "Please! I beg you! Let my brother stay with me!" Victor begged. The guards forced him into a jail like cell that had hay on the floor. They slammed the gates closed and locked them. Victor slid over to the bars. "Please! I beg you!" he called. The guards walked from the building. "Please!" he screamed shaking the bars violently. He rested his head against the bars as he watched them close the door behind them.

Gabriel sat in the truck along with the dead bodies piled in the back. He watched a guard step into the truck and pour gasoline on the bodies and then slowly dumped it over Gabriel's shoulders, arms and legs. Gabriel slowly sat in the corner. "I'm sorry kid," the guard said. Gabriel looked up at him.

"So am I," he whispered. The guard shook his head and stepped down off the truck. Gabriel slowly lowered his head as the guard shut the back tailgate and locked it. Gabriel could feel the darkness closing in around him.

Victor leaned against the bars. He could hear the men that had been sitting across from him laughing. He looked over at them slowly. "That was a fine piece of meat!" they called.

Kyle watched Victor. "Don't listen to them." he called. Victor glanced back at the small opening in the wall. He watched the truck as the guards surround it with torches.

"Whatever you see my friend, know that God has not forsaken you," Victor called to Kyle.

Kyle frowned. "What's going on?" he called.

"The enemy's power is strong, but God's power is much more powerful," Victor said moving towards the gate door.

The guards walked over to the truck and threw the torches under it. The flames climbed the side of the truck and consumed it as the guards surrounded it watching. "Where are the marshmallows?" One of the guards called as the others laughed. The truck was now completely consumed by fire. Suddenly the windows began to vibrate on the buildings and the roof began to tremble loudly. The guards became silent as they looked around slowly. They stared at the truck as the wind began to pick up. Suddenly the flames shot out from the truck knocking the guards to the ground. One of the men glanced back and gasped as Gabriel rose slowly on the truck bed surrounded by flames. "What the…" He whispered, rising. The shackles slid from the Gabriel's wrists. Gabriel stepped slowly through the fire and stepped down from the truck. The guards watched in horror as Gabriel moved away from the truck towards the buildings. The guards remained motionless as they watched in fear.

Victor smiled as the doors of the building were thrown open. Suddenly the wind swept through the building. The locks fell from the cells and the doors opened. "Hey! What about us?" the man that had sat across from them in the truck, yelled. Gabriel walked over to the cell that was still locked and knelt down.

"Only God can forgive those for their sins," Gabriel said. He rose slowly and walked away from cell.

"Oh, come on!" The man called. Gabriel glanced over as Victor stepped out of his cell. He quickly grabbed a coat and handed one to Gabriel.

"Were they scared?" Victor asked.

"Just a little stunned," Gabriel grinned.

"How did you do that?" Kyle asked. Gabriel looked back at him, then over at Victor. "There's a lot of things you won't understand," he began as he could hearing shouting outside and guards racing to the buildings. "Right now, go with them," Victor said pointing to the others who were hurrying from their cells.

"But all the Bibles were destroyed!" Kyle said.

"You'll find more, make sure you get them and hand them to those who are with you and find others, but be safe," Victor said.

Kyle nodded and hurried with the others running from the buildings. Gabriel walked over to the men who were still locked in their cells. The men stared at him. "You can still change. There's still time," Gabriel said. The men shook their heads.

"When we get out of here we will hunt you down!" the man snapped. Gabriel moved away from the cell and quickly followed Victor away from the building. Victor glanced back as the prisoners escaped through the ripped open fence. The guards were still struggling to their feet and in shock from what had just happened.

Victor and Gabriel raced from the fence and stopped seeing a guard's horse standing nearby. Victor ran over to the horse and grabbed the reins. He pulled himself unto the saddle and reached down for Gabriel. He quickly pulled Gabriel unto the horse behind him. They both watched the camp as the shouting of guards suddenly filled the air. Victor turned the horse and quickly fled into the darkness.

CHAPTER FOUR

The horse trotted down the trail through the woods. "Do you think everyone got away?" Gabriel asked.

"I hope so," Victor said guiding the horse forward. The air was damp through the darkness of the woods. Gabriel looked around them as the horse splashed through the puddles of mud. Gabriel looked up in the trees and could see crows sitting among the branches watching them from above. Several vultures landed on the branches and watched as they waited for a free meal.

"I miss the warmth of the sun," Gabriel whispered remembering how in Heaven it was only sunlight, there were never clouds, or rain, only the beauty of the blue sky.

"Me too," Victor said as he watched forward. The branches were intertwined above them blocking out the view of the night sky. Rays of light from the moon managed to peak through thinner branches giving the trail an eerie glow. Victor glanced over feeling something watching them from the darkness of the woods.

"We're being followed," Gabriel whispered seeing shadows move.

"Just focus forward," Victor said. Gabriel continued to watch in front of him. Victor pulled the horse to a stop as the birds in the trees were spooked and flew away. Victor listened to the woods, listening for any movement or change in the air, but there was nothing. He slowly continued forward.

"Are you afraid brother?" Gabriel asked.

"No," Victor said. He pulled the horse to a stop and glanced back at Gabriel, "and neither should you." Gabriel nodded. Victor turned back and continued forward.

"It's just that this world is a strange place. So much sin and so much hate, how do humans do it? How do they survive?" Gabriel asked.

Victor shook his head. "I don't know. I wish I did. It's hard to understand."

"I'm sorry I allowed evil into the garden," Gabriel said.

"It's not your fault, our brother is wise and he'll stop at nothing," Victor said staring forward. "Now hold your tongue, we don't want to give away our position." Gabriel continued to hold on to Victor's shirt.

Morning came slowly but it was still dark and damp in the woods. A slight mist covered the trail around them. The woods remained dark even though the sun was on the brink of rising. Gabriel looked over at the sight of a shadow moving through the woods. "Brother!" he called. Victor pulled back on the reins as several shadows moved into the darkness and disappeared.

"Don't worry, they're staying in the shadows," he said continuing forward. Gabriel continued to watch the woods as they rode along the trail. Finally the trail came through the edge of the woods. Victor pulled the horse to a stop and glanced around. Mountain ranges surrounded them on all sides. Each of the mountains was covered in snow on their tallest peak. Victor could see a road just across the field. He forced the horse forward and rode up to the road.

"Hold on," Gabriel said. He slid down from the saddle and walked over to the road. Kneeling down he slid his fingers across the pavement. He rose as he glanced back at Victor. "Tire tracks, Jared and Anastasia went this way," he said.

"At least we're keeping up with them," Victor said. Gabriel frowned as he walked back over to the horse.

Victor grabbed his arm and pulled him on the horse behind him.

They continued down the long deserted road for most of the day. Victor could see a city ahead. The tall buildings were dark and there were no sounds of cars from inside the city. He sighed, knowing the horse was exhausted from walking all night and both he and Gabriel could use a rest as well.

Night had come as they rode into the city. Victor looked around slowly as they entered the center of the city. The buildings were empty and there appeared to be no signs of life.

"Where is everyone?" Gabriel asked as they continued forward. Victor shook his head finding it strange that no one had been left behind. They came to a building and stopped, seeing that the windows were shattered and most of the merchandise had been stolen.

"It must have been chaos here when the rapture happened," Victor said. Gabriel looked around and saw that all of the buildings were empty. "Looks like no one is here, we'll take cover here for the night," Victor said. He took Gabriel's arm and helped him slide down from the horse. Victor slid down from the saddle and glanced over at a building close by. They entered the building, pulling the horse along with them.

In what use to be a grocery store, Victor tied the horse to a stand outside the door and pulled the saddle from its back. Gabriel pushed the other stands aside and made a clean area for them to set up a fire and to sit. Victor searched through several of the stands and found bags of oats. He opened them and poured them into a sand castle bucket. He set it in front of the horse and walked over to where Gabriel was starting a fire with matches he had found. "Hold on a second," Victor said seeing that there were sprinklers on the ceiling. He walked over to the fire alarm and saw that it was ripped off the wall. "Go ahead," he called. Gabriel sat a pile of newspapers and woods bundled together beside them as Victor sat up blankets and food, such as bread, and some cans that had been left over. Gabriel sat down slowly on his coat and rubbed his hands together. Victor ripped open a package of beef jerky and handed Gabriel a slice.

"Thanks," Gabriel said taking it and eating. Victor slowly rubbed his hands together over the flames. "Do you think they made it to the east coast already?" Gabriel asked.

"Probably, they have the car and the weapons, so I'm sure they're safe," Victor said. Gabriel nodded.

"I'm going to go see if I can find any wood or anything around this town," Gabriel said rising.

"Be careful," Victor said. Gabriel nodded and stepped out from the building. Victor looked around the store slowly, nervous about what or who could be hiding in the darkness.

Outside Gabriel rubbed his arms in the cool night trying to stay warm. He walked down the alley and found several small, thick sticks. He gathered them quickly and rose. He turned back hearing talking and singing close by. He continued down the alley and stopped when he heard the singing getting louder and the laughing mixed with it. Slowly he laid the sticks down and walked over to a boarded up window that was down at the basement level of the building. Kneeling down, he looked through the crack in the boards over the window.

There was a group of people sitting around the room looking forward at a board. Gabriel stared at the chalkboard and could see verses written on it, like John 3:16 and Romans 3:23. He smiled, seeing people reading Bibles. He was relieved to see that some Bibles had survived, where most of them had been burnt and destroyed. He smiled, hearing the singing of hymns. He wanted to join in the praise of his father but he knew that they would be startled. He rose slowly and grabbed the newspapers and sticks and hurried back to the store.

He entered the store with a smile. "I saw people!" he said. Victor looked over at him.

"How far out did you go? Were you followed?" he asked looking at the windows.

"No!" Gabriel said laying the items down. "They were worshipping God. They had Bibles, they had verses on the board."

Victor smiled. "Where were they?" he asked.

"Down that alley over there," Gabriel said pointing out the window.

"Stay here," Victor said. Gabriel nodded as Victor hurried from the store. Gabriel laid several sticks on the fire and rubbed his hands over the flames.

Victor hurried down the alley and stopped, hearing the singing and talking. He knelt down slowly and looked through the crack in the boards. He could hear them laughing and worshipping. The man in front was reading from the Bible. Victor smiled, knowing there was some hope for the people that had been left behind. He slowly rose and hurried back towards the building they were staying in. He entered the building and saw Gabriel look over at him. "At least there's still some hope," he said.

Gabriel smiled. "Should we talk to them?" he asked.

"No, we don't want to scare them," Victor said, walking over to the fire and sitting down on the blanket. Gabriel watched the flames slowly flicker in the breeze. Victor held up his hands to the fire and rubbed them together. "You should lay down and get some rest, we have more traveling tomorrow," he said. Gabriel frowned and slowly lied down. He rested his head down on a bag of seed he had found in the back of the store. Victor slowly lied down and they soon drifted off into a deep sleep.

As the night continued, Victor rolled on his side and continued to sleep. "Victor," came a soft whisper from across the store. "Michael!" the whisper continued. "Michael…wake up," the whisper said. Victor woke slowly and stared at the broken window. "Michael," came another whisper. Victor sat up and looked back at Gabriel. Gabriel was still in a deep sleep. Victor slowly moved his blanket aside and pulled out a dagger. He rose and stopped seeing a figure in the darkness of the store. The figure was that of a small child, not much older than eleven. "Come here Michael," she said holding out her hand. Victor shook his head.

"You cannot fool me," he snapped.

"My father wants to speak to you," she said. "Come!" Victor continued to aim the dagger at her. "Don't be shy," she spoke, holding out her hand as she smiled. The girl looked down at Gabriel then at Victor.

"I'll speak to him, but you leave my brother unharmed," Victor said walking towards her.

"Of course!" she said. Victor walked up to her. "After you," the girl said.

"No, after you," Victor said. The young girl walked up the steps. Victor looked over at Gabriel and saw that he was still asleep. He continued up the steps slowly.

He and the girl entered a room. There was nothing in the room but a chair. A dark figure was sitting in the chair. "He is here as you wished," the girl said.

"Good, now sit," the dark figure demanded. The girl crawled on all fours over to the corner and sat like a dog. Victor watched her then looked over at the figure.

"Damien, so you finally made it," Victor said. Damien laughed softly.

"Indeed," Damien said rising. He had on a long black coat and had dark hair. His skin was pale white. "So…you came a long way I hear," Damien said. "Your brother still at your side like a little lost puppy," he said.

"Leave him out of this," Victor said. "This is between you and me!"

"You cannot stop me," Damien said. "This world will be mine."

"You cannot have what is not yours," Victor demanded.

"Is this really about you and me? Or is it about the people that you protect?" Damien said sharply. "The ones that ate from the tree. The ones who disobeyed our father!"

"They disobeyed our father because of our brother!" Victor snapped. Damien laughed. The girl laughed loudly along with him.

"Silence!" Damien shouted. The girl became quiet instantly. Damien looked at him. Victor watched as Damien walked over to the window and looked out. "Such a lovely night," he said. "Good night for some hunting," Damien said. "I heard there were some Christians close by. I'm sure the guards would like to know."

"Leave them alone!" Victor demanded.

Damien turned to him. "You're living as a human, you actually think you can stop me?" he asked. "What are you going to do? Bring in your army?" he asked. He walked away slowly and smiled. "Oh! I forgot they're not here!" Victor stared at him as Damien turned back. "Or...I could just get rid of the kid downstairs. Send him back to Heaven with a message," Damien growled. Victor pulled a dagger from his coat. "Now... we wouldn't want to do that would we?" Damien said. "There is already a warrant out for you by the guards that your brother terrified with that blow the fire away from you trick," Damien said laughing. "You angels got it all covered, nothing can stop you!" He said. "But I know one way I can."

"Hello Victor," Claudia said from the corner. Damien smiled.

"She's lovely," he said. Victor continued to stare forward at him. "Don't even want to look?" Damien asked. He shook his head slowly. "That figures," he said. "Maybe this will change your mind!" he said.

"No!" came a scream from downstairs. Victor continued to stare forward.

"What? No reaction?" Damien said.

"You can't expect me to fall for your witchcraft and sorcery," Victor snapped.

"Let me guess you're immune to me?" Damien stepping close to him. He slowly whispered in his ear and smiled. "Too bad the screams you are hearing down-stairs, they're not made up," he said. Victor looked at him. "The guards came quickly after receiving a call that Christians had taken up shelter in an abandoned building," Damien said as the sound of trucks could be heard not too far away. Victor raced from the room as Damien smiled.

Victor entered the first floor with his dagger. "Gabe!" he shouted. He stopped when he saw Gabriel still asleep and the fire still burning slowly. "Gabe, wake up!" he called hurrying over to the fire and putting it out. Gabriel sat up slowly and looked at him.

"What's wrong?" he asked.

"We have to go now," Victor said quickly grabbing his bag. Gabriel rose slowly and rolled up the blanket.

"What's wrong?" Gabriel asked again.

"Guards are coming," Victor said hurrying over to the horse and grabbing the saddle. He grabbed the horn of the saddle and place it on the horse's back.

"How did they know where we were?" Gabriel asked hurrying over and handing him the bag.

"Let's just say our cover was blown," Victor said tightening the straps on the saddle.

They rode the horse out into the street and stopped as they glanced over at the entrance of the city. Through the darkness Victor could see six horses standing side by side watching them. The riders were dressed in dark clothes blending in with the darkness around them. Victor watched them, studying the men's forms. They wore black capes with hoods over their heads and their faces partially blocked by cloth. Victor turned the horse and rode from the city as the men sat motionless on the horses, watching.

One of the men looked over at the leader. "Should we follow sir?" He asked.

"No, we have other things we need to take care of," the man said as they rode into the town.

The demon that had once taken the form of a young girl, squealed loudly as the men dragged it into the street by its arms and it's very thin hair. It looked around as it hissed loudly then looked forward at the leader as he stepped in front of the demon. "What do you want from me?" it howled and hissed.

"Damien. Where is he?" the leader called.

"I...I don't know, he vanished!" the demon called. It cocked its head as it looked at the men around it. "You're following those fools aren't you?" it called. The leader hit the demon, knocking it to the ground.

"Watch your tongue, you snake!" the man snapped. The demon stared at him. The men watched the demon. "Well, you're no help to me now," the leader said. He nodded at the men as he walked away.

"No! No! Wait!" The demon howled. The leader looked back. "Damien is going to Washington DC. The new leader is coming to terms with his new responsibility!" the demon called. "Since the president is no longer there…there has to be a new leader!" The demon looked at the men then at the leader. "Please! Please spare me!" it called. The leader stood silently.

"Too bad you've told me what I already know," he said. The demon gasped in horror as the leader nodded and continued to walk away.

"No!" the demon screamed as the men surrounded it. The leader looked back slowly as fire slowly rose from where the demon had been sitting. The men walked towards him and stopped.

"What do we do now?" one of the men asked.

"We head to Washington, we'll meet up with them there," the leader said, walking back to his horse and climbing up on the saddle. They quickly rode out of the city and into the darkness.

Gabriel sat on the horse behind Victor as they rode through the woods. He dreaded being back in the woods on the trail. There were plenty of hiding spots in the woods. Victor watched ahead as the horse moved forward. "I wish it were day," Gabriel said. "That way we could see the beauty of the woods." Victor groaned as he stared forward. Victor stopped, hearing the click of a gun. Glancing over he saw a man standing behind a tree with his rifle aimed at them.

"We will not hurt you," Victor said.

"How do I know that?" the man asked.

"We escaped from a camp about a day back. We're heading towards Washington DC," Victor said.

"To help that new leader?" the man asked remaining in the shadows.

"No, we're heading there to travel across the seas to fight the war," Victor said.

"That boy looks too young to fight," the man said, continuing to remain beside the tree.

"He is older than you think," Victor said. "Will you please put your rifle down, we mean no harm."

"What is your name sir?" the man asked.

"Victor, this is my brother Gabriel," Victor said. Gabriel watched the man silently. "What is your name?" Victor asked.

"My name is Tony," the man said lowering his rifle. "My wife that has been left behind, has taken up shelter not too far from here. We found it safe enough out of the way from those soldiers. You two look exhausted," he said. "I live not too far from here if you would like to stay the night and rest and have something to eat."

"Sounds fair enough," Victor said with a nod. Tony walked from the shadows and unto the trail. He was dressed in an army uniform. "You're part of the military?" Victor asked.

"I was," Tony said with a nod. "Up until two days ago when they found out I was a new born again Christian. Then they kicked me out."

"That's awful," Gabriel whispered.

"It's okay, I mean I have a family here and she is born again. We'll be ready when Christ returns with his kingdom," Tony said with a nod.

"That's all that matters," Victor said. Tony walked with them down the trail. They came to a small house. The lights were off inside but they could see the small glow of a fire in the fireplace. Gabriel slid down from the horse as Tony walked over to the door and knocked twice then one time. A young woman opened the door and stopped, seeing Victor and Gabriel. Gabriel stood close to Victor.

"Why did you bring them here?" the woman asked.

"They're going to the middle east to fight in the war. They're soldiers just like me," Tony said. The woman looked back at them. Her long blonde hair seemed to have not been washed in several days. She looked at Tony and sighed heavily and nodded as she moved away from the door. Victor tied the horse to a branch and entered the house with Tony and Gabriel.

As night continued, Victor stood watching out the window. The woman walked over to him and handed him a bowl of soup. Victor looked at her and nodded as he took the bowl slowly. "My name is Rebecca," she said.

Victor smiled. "Friends call me Victor, but my real name is Michael," he replied. "That's my brother Gabriel."

"Good Biblical names, those are the names of angels," Rebecca said. Victor nodded as he took a sip of the soup. He sighed at the taste and warmth of it.

"This is really good," he said. Rebecca smiled at the compliment.

"It's made from homegrown vegetables," she said.

"You're a good cook," he said. Rebecca smiled as she returned to the living room. Victor glanced back out the window as he continued to eat the soup.

Gabriel sat on a blanket in the front of the fireplace. Tony handed him a bowl of soup. "Thanks," Gabriel said taking a sip of the soup. Tony sat down beside him. "So...you're a soldier?" he asked.

"Yeah, I still am," Gabriel replied.

"How old are you?" Tony asked.

"Seventeen," Gabriel said.

"I didn't even know that they allowed seventeen year olds into the military," Tony said.

"Where we are from, they start early," Victor said entering the room and sitting down on the couch.

"And where exactly are you from?" Tony asked.

"Up north," Gabriel said quickly.

"Were your weapons taken?" Tony asked.

"They were taken by some friends for safety, they are going to meet us in the east," Victor said.

"A lot of the soldiers I worked with turned," Tony said.

"Turned?" Gabriel asked.

"They....they are no longer for the free nation," Tony said. "They just turned away from what they were really fighting for," Tony said.

"Do you think that they would come back and join the fight?" Victor asked.

"I don't know. I wish they would," Tony said. "God is worth fighting for."

"There will be a war, many nations will come together to fight," Victor said. Gabriel looked over at him then at Tony. "The armies will be strong and have many men," Victor said.

"How do you know this?" Tony asked.

"Because it's my army," Victor said.

"Do you work for the government or something?" Tony asked.

"No, I work for God," Victor replied.

"How were you not taken during the rapture? Are you a born again believer?" Tony asked. Gabriel looked over at Victor.

"I guess you could put it like that," Victor said. Gabriel ate his soup slowly as he listened to the conversation between Victor and Tony. He remembered back to the time God had called on him...

Gabriel walked down the stone walkway towards the throne. He slowly knelt down before God. "Yes father?"

he whispered. He rose as he stared at the light before him. He listened and nodded. "I will tell her, I understand father," he said with a nod. He walked down the stone walk way back to the gates.

Gabriel entered the small village in Nazareth. Glancing around he watched sheep roam freely and people going about their business. He stopped, seeing a young woman walking to a small house with a basket of wheat. She was the one...the one that would be the mother of God's son.

Entering her house, Mary laid her basket down and turned, hearing the wind blow through the small house. She listened for any other movement. Slowly she returned to her basket. Behind her she could feel someone watching from the door. Turning back she gasped seeing a figure at the doorway. His beauty had never been seen before. His crystal blue eyes and flawless skin seemed unearthly. She stepped back slowly, for being seen with another man could get her killed. "Hail, thou that art highly favoured, the Lord is with thee: blessed art thou among women," Gabriel said. "Fear not, Mary: for thou hast found favor with God. And behold, thou shalt conceive in thy womb, and bring forth a son, and shalt call his name JESUS. He shall be great, and shall be called the Son of the Highest: and the Lord God shall give unto him the throne of his father David: And he shall reign over the house of Jacob forever; and of his kingdom there shall be no end." Gabriel said. His voice was smooth like the sound of a gentle breeze. Mary shook her head, disturbed by what she was hearing.

"How could this be? I know not a man," she said.

"The Holy Ghost shall come upon thee, and the power of the Highest shall overshadow thee: therefore also that holy thing which shall be born of thee shall be called the Son of God," Gabriel said. She turned back to the basket and stood silently. Turning back she stopped, seeing that Gabriel was now gone.

Gabriel broke from the dream as Tony's wife took his empty bowl. He nodded. "Thank you," he said. Rebecca smiled and returned to the kitchen. Victor sat on the couch silently.

"How long will this war last?" Tony asked.

Victor looked at Gabriel then at Tony and his wife. "This war has been happening for many centuries. People just haven't been able to see it," Victor said. Gabriel looked back at the flames in the fireplace as Victor continued. "The next seven years the war will grow, once the seventh year comes, no land will be untouched."

Tony and his wife looked at each other. "Will he be called to war?" Rebecca asked. Victor looked at Tony.

"It will be against his own will, but yes, he will fight in the battle," Victor replied.

Tony rose slowly and nodded. "Then I will serve my God," he said. Gabriel looked up at him then back at Victor.

"This war will not be easy," Victor said.

Gabriel rose slowly. "But in the end God will prevail," he said.

"That's why I will fight, I know good men that will fight alongside you and your men," Tony said.

Victor frowned. "When you are called, do not fear, God will be with you."

"You should get rest if you want to leave early," Tony said. Victor nodded and laid down slowly on the couch. Gabriel sat down beside the fire and watched the flames as they flickered slowly. Tony sat down beside him as Victor watched them from the couch.

"I never imagined being left behind," Tony said. Gabriel looked at him. "I just…didn't believe. Then this happens and I come to a shocking conclusion that I was blind." He looked at Gabriel then back at the flames. "You're young, you probably haven't seen much battle."

"Have you?" Gabriel asked. "Have you seen many wars?"

"The war in Iraq and in Afghanistan. I watched friends die right before my eyes," Tony frowned. Gabriel looked back at Victor who was now asleep.

"I fought alongside my brothers. It wasn't easy," he said.

"What branch?" Tony asked, interested in knowing how one so young could be in war.

"We were ground soldiers," Gabriel answered.

"Must have been the army or marines," Tony said.

Gabriel looked back at the fire and sighed. "It was hard," he said continuing to stare forward.

Tony looked over at him. "For a teenager, it is hard. It's something they should never have to see," he said.

Gabriel looked over at him. "No adult should ever have to see it either," he said.

"But it's what we do, we're trained to fight for our country," Tony said.

"My brothers and I weren't trained, we were created to fight…to protect and serve," Gabriel said. "The hardest part was fighting against my own brother."

"You fought against your brother?" Tony asked.

Gabriel nodded. "He turned against us," Gabriel said. "He fought against us. He killed his own brothers."

"That's awful," Tony replied.

"That's my brother, he'll stop at nothing," Gabriel said.

"Sounds like a dictator, hate to be under his rule," Tony said. Gabriel looked over at him. He knew that day would come soon enough.

"I better get some sleep," he said walking over to the recliner and sitting down in it. He continued to watch the fire in the fireplace as he rested his head on the arm rest. He watched Tony remain in front of the fireplace. He knew that Tony had seen a lot of war, and it wasn't his place to ask him to fight in this war. Gabriel shut his eyes trying to put himself away from the coming war and the pain that was soon to follow.

CHAPTER FIVE

At the White House, Mason walked down the long hall towards the Oval Office. Since the rapture the congress had been in a state of panic. It was his job to keep everyone calm and make sure everything was being done to help those affected. He entered the Oval Office and shut the door. As he walked over to the desk he sighed heavily seeing the mountain of paperwork. He looked through the paperwork, he stopped as he heard clawing at the door. Slowly he lowered his pen as he looked at the shut door. The scratching stopped. Shaking his head he went back to reading the paperwork. He stopped again hearing scratching and clawing at the door. Rising he walked over to the door and opened it slowly. There was nothing at the door. "Hey Tonya, did anyone bring any animals in?" he called to the secretary.

"No sir," Tonya replied rising.

"Okay, thank you," he said shutting the door. He turned back and stopped, seeing Damien sitting in the chair in the corner of the room. "How on earth did you sneak by me?" Mason asked. Damien smiled as he cleaned under his nails with a sharp letter opener.

"Didn't take much!" Damien said sitting forward.

"I'm sorry, I have a lot to do," Mason said as he sat down in his desk chair. Damien smiled as he looked back down at his hand.

"You know splinters take forever to get out," he said holding up his hand. There were thousands of splinters sticking out of his skin. Mason looked back at him as he lowered his pen. "Look, did you set up an appointment with Tonya?" he asked.

"I don't need an appointment. This office will suit me just fine," Damien said.

"Sorry, this office has been filled," Mason said continuing to read through paperwork. Damien rose slowly and looked around the office.

"You know I can help you run this country, and all countries if you allow me," he said.

"I'm not about ruling the world you know," Mason said.

"But…what if you could?" Damien said with a smile. Mason grinned as he stared at Damien. "The world is in crisis right now, people are frightened and scared, they need a leader that can control that fear," Damien said. Mason sat back in his chair.

"That sounds like world domination," he said.

"Exactly!" Damien said with a smile. "What chance does the world have when it's in a state of panic?"

"The world leaders will never allow me to do such a thing," Mason said.

"That's why we get rid of the leaders and make it where the world is under one rule," Damien said.

"I'm sorry, I can't," Mason said. Damien stood watching him. "Please, feel free to see yourself out," Mason said turning back to his paperwork. Damien stared at him feeling defeated and that wasn't something he was going to let happen. He leaned against the desk.

"Well, I tried, I thought this would be a partnership that would work well in the end," he said. "I was sadly mistaken." Mason continued to work as Damien walked to the door. He stopped as he slowly locked it. Mason looked up at him. "So sad it had to end this way," Damien said, turning back and walking over to the desk. Damien jumped up unto the desk and landed on his hands and feet. Mason jerked back in horror. He quickly rose and raced for the door. He struggled to unlock it but it wouldn't budge. He jerked back and saw that Damien was gone. He raced over to his desk and dialed a number to the secretary's desk. He stopped and looked down at the phone and saw that it was dead. He heard clawing sounds at the door. Racing over to the closet he got in and shut the doors. He breathed heavily as he listened for movement as he peaked through the crack between the doors of the closet. He could hear growling and the sound of something dragging across the floor.

"Come out!" came a deep growl. Mason gasped as he moved away from the door. He could feel the cold chill coming between the doors. Fear overwhelmed him as he looked away. "I just want to speak to you," came another growl as he could hear claws scratch at the closet doors. He shouted in horror as the doors shook violently. He could hear the wood tearing away as the claws dug into the door violently. Covering his ears, he watched in horror as the door continued to shake. Suddenly it stopped. He lowered his hands as he listened for any movement coming from outside the closet. He slowly peeked through the crack in the door and watched. There was no movement in the office that he could see. Slowly he opened the door and looked around the office. The office was now empty. He stepped from the closet and raced over to the door and struggled to unlock it.

"Open the doors!" he screamed pounding on it. He jerked back seeing a dark figure standing at the window watching out. "What do you want from me?" he screamed. The figure continued to stare out the window. "Please! Tell me! What do you want?" Mason screamed.

"The days of darkness have fallen upon us," the dark figure said. He slowly glanced back as the shadow covered his face. "We will claim this land and all that belongs to it." Mason turned back and struggled to unlock the door. Slowly the wood on the door began to chip away like claws digging into it. Mason stepped away from the door as three numbers slowly emerged through the chipped away paint.

"No! No!" Mason whispered as 666 appeared on the door. Tears streamed down his face as he turned back to the figure. "I don't want this!" he shouted. The figure continued to watch out the window. Mason falls to his knees as he sobs. "Please, I beg you!" he begged. The figure slowly walked towards him and knelt down.

"You fall to your knees before me? You will serve my master as your God," he growled. He forced Mason on his back. Mason screamed as he kicked and thrashed violently as the figure leaned over him.

The door was opened as Mason rolled on his side. He glanced back seeing that the numbers were no longer noticeable on the door. Tonya entered with several security members. "Are you alright?" Tonya asked. Mason rose and straightened his tie. He glanced back at her and smiled.

"I'm fine," he said. Tonya glanced around the office and saw the chairs knocked over and papers scattered.

"Are you sure?" she asked.

"Do you question me?" Mason asked.

"No, no sir!" Tonya said.

"Then leave me, I have things to do," Mason said returning to his desk. Tonya nodded and started out the door. "Before you leave, can you send in Danny and Brandon?" Tonya nodded and left the room. He looked down at the paper work on the desk. Slowly he crumpled it up and threw it away in the trashcan.

Two marines entered the office and stood at attention in front of the desk. Mason stopped writing and looked up at them. "I believe out of respect you should knock," he snapped. "Leave and return," he snapped. Danny and Brandon looked at one another then at Mason. "Do I need to repeat myself?" Mason asked sharply.

"No sir," Brandon said. They both left the office. Mason sat back as there came a knock on the door.

"Enter!" he called. The two soldiers entered the office and stood at attention. Mason rose and walked over to them. "Two strong military men, the future of our country and everything it stands for. What exactly do our military fight for?"

"For our freedom!" Danny said.

"That freedom is no longer an option," Mason said. Brandon and Danny looked at each other and then over at him. "The world today is no longer free and is no longer under the control of the people. I have the control and I will make the rules that the people will live by and if they don't, they will be punished by the law," Mason said walking to the window.

"But sir…the people have the right to decide," Danny said. Mason glanced back at him.

"You honestly think they are capable of that?" he asked. "Capable of making the right choices? Capable of making goals?" He laughed as he paced in front of them. "The world is no longer a guessing game. My policy will make them see that I have the best choices for them and if they don't follow….they will be punished." Danny stared at him then looked at Brandon. "Do we have a problem?" Mason asked.

"Sir, no sir," Brandon said.

"There is something you must do for me," Mason said stepping in front of Brandon. Brandon was the younger of the two at twenty-five years old. Danny was in his early forties. Mason slowly slid his hand down the front of the marine's uniform and yanked off the metal. "You won't need this," Mason said dropping it into the trash. Danny stared at Mason. "You will go and retrieve the flag," Mason said. "Don't keep me waiting." Brandon nodded and hurried from the office. Mason turned to Danny. Danny stared forward.

"You have no right to strip that boy of that metal. He earned it!" he snapped. Mason laughed softly.

"He earned nothing!" He snapped. "I have a job for you!" Danny looked forward.

"What would you have me do?" he asked.

"The cemetery…get rid of the crosses," Mason said returning to his desk. Danny stared at him.

"But sir…." he began. Mason slammed his fist against the desk.

"There will be no talking back to me!" he shouted. Danny sank back. "Get rid of them!" Mason shouted. Danny nodded slowly and walked from the office.

Danny walked down the sidewalk from the White House. He watched Brandon walking towards him. "You don't have to do this," Danny said.

"It was an order, an order from our leader," Brandon said.

"He's not our leader," Danny said. Brandon held the folded American flag. "I don't know who that is in there," Danny said. He slowly slid the metal off his coat and placed it in Brandon's hand and closed his fingers around it.

"I can't take this," Brandon said shaking his head.

"We fought side by side, we earned this metal," Danny said. "You earned this metal. Don't let him strip it from you." Danny looked down at the Purple Heart. He slowly handed it back to Danny.

"Hold on to it for me?" He asked. Danny nodded, as he started down the sidewalk. "Will we meet again?" Brandon called.

"Americans won't stand for this, we will meet again my brother on the battlefield and there we will claim our victory," Danny called. Brandon nodded as Danny continued down the sidewalk. Brandon sighed heavily and continued towards the White House.

Danny slowly walked over to the cemetery and stopped. He sighed and slowly entered the gates. He walked down the green grass staring at the tombstones as he walked. He could see cross marked on each tombstone. Removing the cross would require destroying each and every tombstone. Most of the buried were military men and women. He stopped in front of one gravestone and knelt down. Tears stream down his face as he stared at his father's name just above the cross. "Dad, what do I do?" he whispered. "This isn't our leader! He will destroy this great nation," he whispered. Slowly a hand pressed down on his shoulder. He glanced back and rose seeing an elderly man before him. "Who are you?" Danny whispered.

"A friend," the elderly man said. "There is a war coming. All nations feel it. No one can stop it. There is an army growing in the east," the elderly man said. "They will be unstoppable against this evil, for God is with them." Danny looked down at his father's tombstone.

"How…?" Danny glanced back and stopped, seeing the elderly man was no longer there. He sighed and looked back at the White House. He quickly hurried from the cemetery and back to the White House.

Brandon knocked on the door to the Oval Office. "Enter," Mason called from behind the door. Brandon entered with the flag. "Ah…you have it," Mason said. Brandon handed him the folded flag. Mason unfolded the flag and cringed. He dumped the trash unto the floor and sat the trashcan down.

"Sir…" Brandon began. He gasped as Mason dropped the flag into the trashcan and pulled out a lighter. Mason dropped the lighter. Brandon stepped back as the trashcan erupted into flames. Mason smiled as he watched the flames. Brandon stared at trashcan in anger. He sadly watched the flag burn. It was a disgrace to the nation and all that lived there. "Is there anything else you would like me to do?"

Mason looked at him and smiled.

"Bring the rest," he said. Brandon frowned and sadly walked from the office.

Brandon hurried from the White House as Danny raced over to him. "We're leaving," Danny said.

"What?" Brandon said. "We can't!"

"I can't stay here," Danny said. "Either you're with me, or you're against me."

Brandon stared at him. "He just torched the American flag," he whispered. "How can our own leader do such a terrible act?"

"Because he's not our leader. He told me to get rid of the crosses in the cemetery," Danny said.

"Did you?" Brandon asked.

"No," Danny said. "While I was there this elderly man came to me, he spoke of a war coming. Armies are gathering in the east, armies that will fight against this evil. I'm going," he said. He started back down the sidewalk. Brandon stood motionless knowing he didn't want to return to the White House. He glanced back slowly at the White House then at Danny. "Well?" Danny said. Brandon nodded slowly.

"I'm coming with you," he said. Danny nodded as the two of them hurried down the sidewalk.

Mason watched from the window in anger. Slowly he slid the curtains closed. He walked over to his desk and sat down. "Tonya, come to my office," he said over the phone. Tonya entered the office.

"Yes sir," she said as she walked up to the desk. Mason looked up at her.

"A new law is about be sent to the senate, I want them all there and prepare to take a vote," Mason said. Tonya agreed and hurried from the office. Mason smiled as he sat back in his seat. He was ready to push the world into domination. He would control everything and everyone. He rose slowly from his seat and walked over to the mirror hanging on the wall. He smiled as he fixed his tie. Staring at the mirror he continued to smile as he eyes became sunken in and his face became deathly thin like that of a skeleton.

Gabriel jerked awake with a scream and sat up, seeing Damien's face in his nightmare. Victor rose and raced over to where Gabriel was lying beside the fire. "Are you alright?" he asked. Gabriel stared at the flames in the fireplace.

"He's here," he whispered looking back at Victor. Tony and his wife entered the room.

"Who's here?" Tony asked.

"It was a nightmare," Gabriel said not wanting to worry Tony and his wife.

"Okay," Rebecca said as they slowly went back to their room. Victor sat down next to Gabriel.

"It's going to get worse," Gabriel said.

Victor agreed. "I hope they'll be prepared," he said.

"And if they're not?" Gabriel asked.

"Then we'll do our best to try to make them," Victor said. "Get packed, I'm going to go check on the horse and make sure everything's ready." Gabriel nodded as Victor walked from the house.

In the darkness of the night, Victor entered the small barn. Victor stopped seeing Jared leaning against the door. "Glad you made it," he said walking over to the horse.

"We're in a tough spot," Jared said. Victor looked over at him. "Damien has officially gained control, there's no stopping him now," Jared said. "He's already having the American flags removed and burned, and now it's the crosses and every religious aspect that still remains. He put in place a new law…" Jared began.

"What law is that?" Victor asked.

"You know of the law I speak," Jared said. Victor stared at him. "Kill every new Christian, he will stop at nothing!" Jared said.

"Where are the weapons?" Victor asked placing the saddle on the stable wall.

"They are safe," Jared said. "We managed to get through every road block without a problem." Anastasia appeared at the doorway with a bow and arrow. An arrow was pressed against the string.

"Where is Gabriel?" she asked.

"Inside, why?" Victor asked.

"I was tracking a demon from the road. It disappeared here," Anastasia said. Victor rushed to the door of the barn.

Gabriel slowly packed his belongings in a bag. There was a knock on the door. He listened and waited. He watched the door as Tony came down stairs. "No!" Gabriel called rising.

"What?" Tony asked. Gabriel slowly pulled a dagger from his bag. Tony stared at the dagger and then at Gabriel. "What kind of soldier are you?"

"Don't ask," Gabriel said slowly stepping up to the door. There was another knock at the door. "Go back upstairs, lock the door to your room. Lock all the windows." Tony raced upstairs. Gabriel stood at the door waiting as another knock could be heard. He slowly looked through the peephole but saw no one at the door. He took the doorknob and waited to turn it. The doorknob shook in his hand as loud clawing at the wood of the door could be heard. Breath could be seen blowing from under the door. Gabriel dove away from the door as the door was thrown open. Instantly, the flames in the fire went out as the house became ice cold. Gabriel slid behind the wall and listened as the man entered the cabin.

"Come out, come out, wherever you are!" he growled. He smiled as he slid his claw like fingers along the wall. Another demon entered the house. He sniffed the air and smiled.

"I smell Christians," he whispered to the other. The other sniffed the air and cringed.

"Do you smell that?" he added. The other demon nodded.

"An angel is also here," he snarled. "Find him." The other demon quickly took off down the hall as the lead demon lifted his head and sniffed the air and sneered. He quickly raced up the steps to the bedroom where Tony and his wife had taken shelter.

The demon stopped at the bed room door and slowly slid its claws down the wood. He rested his head against the door and listened to Rebecca's soft cries. "Knock, knock!" Victor said. The demon jerked back as Victor aimed the arrow at the demon and shot it. The demon squirmed and hollered as Victor raced over and tackled him, destroying him with one swipe of a blade. He glanced over at Tony as he stared down at the demon from the doorway.

"What is that?" He asked.

"Trust me, you don't want to know," Victor said rising.

"Where's the kid?" Tony asked, racing past Victor.

Gabriel sat back against the wall listening to the demon's movement. He looked down at the dagger in his hand as he felt the movement of the demon getting closer. He rose from the shadows as the demon turned back and stared at him. "No!" The demon screamed. Gabriel threw the dagger at the demon striking it in the chest. The demon fell to the ground as Tony entered with a rifle. He stopped, seeing the body on the floor. Slowly he lowered the rifle.

"I…I don't understand, what just happened?" Tony asked. Gabriel walked over and took his dagger.

"They're coming," he said, sliding the dagger back into his belt.

"I've read about them. I've never….never in my life encountered a demon," Tony said. Victor walked over and stripped the weapons from the demon.

"Trust me…you will never want to encounter one again," he said. "They were once like us…until they fell." Tony looked over at Victor.

"Like us?" He asked. Gabriel looked over at Victor then back at Tony.

"He means angels," he said. Tony frowned as he watched Victor pack the bags quickly.

"You guys should stay for the rest of the night and head out in the morning," Tony said. Gabriel looked over at Victor silently.

"We have to keep moving," Victor said, zipping the bag up.

"But it's late," Rebecca replied. Victor looked over at Gabriel. Gabriel stood silently staring at the couple, offering their home as shelter. Laying the bag down Victor sighed.

"Okay, we'll wait till morning," he said as Jared and Anastasia entered the home. "Until then, they will stand guard." Tony and Rebecca stared at Jared and Anastasia.

"You must be starving," Rebecca said. "I have some extra soup." She hurried into the kitchen as Anastasia followed. Gabriel knelt down slowly and rolled up his blanket. He glanced over at the table and saw the Bible laying open on it. Tony slowly picked it up and sat down beside him in front of the fireplace.

"I want you to have this," he said. Gabriel looked at the Bible then at Tony. He smiled and shook his head as he pushed it back to him slowly.

"Don't worry about me, I know my father," he said.

Tony rose and entered the kitchen hearing the talking and laughing. Gabriel sat down slowly in front of the fireplace as Victor sat on the couch.

"Do not become close. Many will die in this war," Victor said. Gabriel agreed.

"I know, but they deserve a chance," he said looking back at him.

"They all deserve a chance…but many will fall," Victor said rising slowly and walking to the kitchen. He stopped at the door and looked back at Gabriel.

"The wicked will rise and the chains will be smashed. This is our war," he said. Gabriel looked back at the fire as Victor entered the kitchen shutting the door behind him.

CHAPTER SIX

Gabriel woke to the sound of the television playing. He sat up and saw Tony watching the television as he ate a bowl of oatmeal. "Come look at this!" Tony called. Gabriel rose as the others entered. Victor walked over and stopped, seeing Mason standing at the podium. "Today we will take back our freedom," Mason called as the crowds cheered. "There has to be change, change that will make our nation stronger," he called. Victor looked over Jared.

"This war is coming faster than I had thought," Jared said.

"Today I will meet with the world leaders and we will devise a plan that will bring us together," Mason said as the crowd cheered.

"We have to be moving," Victor said, grabbing the bags and walking outside.

Gabriel walked from the cabin as Victor loaded the bag unto the saddle. He quickly climbed up on the saddle. "Did you get rid of the demons?" he asked. Anastasia nodded.

"Their scent is covered," she called, walking towards the car and getting in. A slight fog had settled over the street going away from the cabin. Jared smiled as Rebecca handed him a thermos of soup.

"Thank you," he said, walking over to the car and getting in. Victor sat on the horse and slowly pulled the shawl over his arms and shoulders. Gabriel slid his shawl on and walked over to the horse. Rebecca handed him a thermos.

"For the road," she smiled. Gabriel smiled back and took the thermos.

"Thank you," he said. Rebecca stepped back away from the horse. Gabriel took Victor's hand and slid up on the horse behind him.

"Make sure you keep an eye out, don't open the door for anyone. You will be called when the time of war is near," Victor said.

"But how will I know?" Tony called.

"Wait for the eagle," Victor called as the horse trotted down the street behind the car. Tony watched as they disappeared into the mist.

The horse trotted slowly through the woods as the car, being driven by Jared, had disappeared. "Can I ask you something?" Gabriel asked.

"Sure," Victor said as he stared ahead.

"Do you think people realize that this man is possessed?" Gabriel asked.

"I don't think it's crossed their minds," Victor replied. "They see him as a savior, one that can bring promise to this land and help ease their sorrow."

"But that won't last long," he said. Victor shook his head.

"Once they see the power he's trying to inflict upon them, they'll figure it out," he said. Gabriel pulled the hood over his head and leaned against Victor struggling to stay warm in the cold winter air. Victor continued to stare forward.

"I wish it was over!" Gabriel whispered.

"Me too brother! Me too," Victor said as they continued through the woods.

As the day continued Victor knelt down beside the stream and took a sip of water from his cupped hands. He glanced back at Gabriel, who was sharpening his blade against a rock. Victor sighed as he glanced back forward. He rose, seeing movement not too far from an opening in the woods. "Gabe!" he called as he raced back towards him. He quickly grabbed the horse's reins and pulled the horse behind the tree. Victor and Gabriel crouched down behind the tree log and branches. They watched as four of the six men rode through the woods.

"They're following us," Gabriel whispered. Victor watched the men ride across the stream and disappeared.

"They've been following us since we left Anastasia's house. We have to go," Victor said, rising quickly. They quickly got on the horse and rode away from the area and disappeared. One of the men walked slowly from the depth of the woods as another one of the men on a horse came over to him.

"They're moving on," one of the men said.

"We'll follow," he said, guiding his horse forward. The other man quickly got back in the saddle and rode along the stream following the leader.

Victor watched ahead along the trail as clouds had moved in and took the sunlight out of the day. He glanced around, listening to the movements and the sounds of animals. Gabriel glanced up at the sound of crows in the branches above them. "It's so still, and quiet," he whispered.

Victor pulled the horse to a stop and listened. He looked up and saw the crows watching them. They both slid down and walked to the edge of the trail. Victor drew his sword from the sheath. "Stay beside the horse," he said pushing Gabriel over to the horse. Gabriel stood beside the horse as Victor walked over to the ground and knelt down. He slowly slid his fingers through the wet mud and rose. "We're being tracked by hounds," he said. Gabriel grabbed his dagger from the bag around the saddle horn. Victor backed away slowly as he gripped his sword. He glanced up at the crows that have now multiplied into twenty birds, lining the tree branches. Victor stepped over to the horse and climbed on. He grabbed Gabriel's arm and pulled him on behind him. Victor continued down the trail as he watched around him. Gabriel watched behind and from side to side as he gripped the dagger.

"I'm not seeing anything," he said, watching for any movement. Victor watched ahead.

"They're keeping in the shadows," he added, seeing faint movement in the darkness. "Let's hope they stay there," Victor said. Gabriel slowly slid his dagger into his belt.

As the days passed, the horse struggled to keep the pace. Gabriel watched the cities burn in the distance as they rode across the plains. Victor watched sadly as they continued. He pulled back on the reins seeing cars passing through a traffic stop area.

"They're going to see us," Gabriel warned.

"You need to go around with the bags," Victor said, throwing his leg over the horse's neck and sliding down from the saddle.

"What about you?" Gabriel asked.

"I'll keep them distracted," Victor said sliding the sword into the bag on the saddle. Gabriel pulled himself forward unto the saddle. Victor gripped Gabriel's hands. "Whatever you do...do not look back, those hounds are close," he frowned. "You keep going."

"No! Not without you!" Gabriel said. The guards could be heard shouting.

"I'll find you," Victor whispered. Gabriel nodded as he turned the horse and charged into the woods. Victor glanced back as the guards raced up to him with weapons drawn. He lifted his hands allowing to the guards to take him.

The woods were dark and a thick fog had settled above the trail. Gabriel gripped the reins as he looked at the woods around him. "Don't worry boy, I'll protect us," he whispered to the horse as he patted its neck. Gabriel glanced back, hearing laughing in the darkness. Birds landed on the branches above them. Gabriel slowly slid the hood over his head as he watched forward and blinding himself to everything around him. Every so often he would catch a glimpse of something hovering in the woods, watching him. He pulled back on the reins seeing shadows moving quickly in the darkness. He glanced back and watched the shadows slowly step unto the trail. "Move forward," he whispered forcing the horse to keep going. "Don't look back." The sound of chirping filled the woods like an echo. He pulled back on the reins and listened as the chirping came from one side of the trail then a response could be heard from ahead. A tree branch snapped and landed with a loud crash in the woods. The horse reared up, causing Gabriel to fall back and land in the mud. He rose as the horse raced through the darkness and disappeared. "No!" he called. He stopped as he looked around. He was now alone and at the mercy of the darkness. There were no weapons for protection. Seeing that he was now alone, he folded his arms and continued forward. Deep down inside he hoped the horse would stop somewhere ahead.

As morning broke, snow began to fall gently around him. The sound of faint sleet filled the trees. Gabriel drifted in and out of sleep as he continued walking. He stepped into a mud puddle covered with ice and fell. He struggled to force himself up but didn't have the strength. He laid motionless on the snow covered ground as the gloomy day continued.

As night fell, so did the temperature. The sounds of horses charging down the trail could be heard coming toward Gabriel. The leader of the group of six men pulled his horse to a stop as he looked down at him. The others came up beside him and stopped. "It's not like him to be alone," one of the men said to another. "Something has happened, he wouldn't have been left like this," The leader looked at the surrounding woods.

"Get him up we'll take him with us," he said. Several of the men slid down from their horses and walked over to Gabriel.

Gabriel woke slowly to the sound of a crackling fire. He stared forward and could see the large fire in front of him. Slowly a warm rag was wrapped around both of his hands. "You're awake, finally," said a strong voice. Gabriel jerked up and saw the six men around the fire. He looked forward at the leader.

"Raphael?" he whispered.

"Long time, brother," the man said pulling down the cloth protecting his face.

"Where's Michael?" Gabriel asked looking down at the cloth around his hands.

"Haven't heard from him. We found you passed out on the trail," Raphael said stirring the fire. Gabriel shook his head.

"He'll be angry with me," he said.

"Why?" Raphael asked.

"I lost the horse and the weapons," Gabriel said.

"That horse?" Raphael asked. Gabriel looked back and saw the horse tied to the tree. Gabriel sighed as he looked back at Raphael.

"You were following us," he said. "You were the one in the shadows," Gabriel said facing the fire and rubbing his hands. Raphael smiled.

"What can I say, I was just watching your back," he said. "Good thing too, you almost lost your fingers from the cold." Gabriel looked down at his fingers and saw that his nails were still blue but the color was slowly returning.

"How bad is Mason?" he asked.

"Bad," Raphael said. "Everything is becoming more and more controlled. We're lucky, we know our way. But humans, they don't get it." Gabriel wrapped the warm rags around his hands and sighed heavily as he held them back over the fire.

"So you came all the way up north from New Orleans?" Gabriel asked.

"That's right, I was told that Michael had arrived and that his brother was with him. There were warnings sent by other angels that the armies were on the move. Positioning themselves for when the call was made, they would gather where the leader commanded," Raphael said. "We had a few close calls, but nothing we can't handle." Gabriel nodded. Raphael took several warm towels from a steaming pot and took the ones from Gabriel's hands. He slowly wrapped the warm ones around them.

"Thanks," Gabriel said. Raphael nodded as he placed the cool clothes in the steaming water. The tip of a sword tapped the back of Raphael's neck. Gabriel rose slowly as Victor appeared from the darkness.

"You know you're always to be prepared," he said. Raphael smiled as he rose. Victor smiled. "It's good to see you brother!" he said. Raphael smiled and hugged him. "Long travel?" he asked.

"You have no idea," Raphael said. "Where have you been?"

"Got stopped at the road block. Nothing I couldn't handle," Victor said. He looked over at Gabriel then down at his hands wrapped in towels. He slowly lifted them up. "What is this?" he said.

"Frost bite," Gabriel said. "It's alright." Victor nodded as he glanced over at the men. He smiled.

"Good evening gentlemen," he called. The men cheered as Gabriel and Raphael smiled. Victor walked over and sat down beside Gabriel on a log. Victor warmed his hands in front of the fire. "What's the word back east?" he asked.

"Mason is having flags burnt, crosses destroyed, churches are closed down. People are taken it upon themselves to have church in their basements. He put in a new law, that people have to receive a mark," Raphael said.

"And if they don't?" Gabriel asked.

"Then its death," Raphael said. Gabriel stared down angrily. "The Christians they find are being gathered. Some are killed, some…are forced to join Mason's army."

"But some will fight in God's army. They will hear the call," Victor said.

"Let's hope so," Raphael said. "We need everyone we can get." He took another bite of a piece of meat from a bird that they had killed along the way.

"Some of the soldiers at the road block had this mark," Victor said holding up a piece of paper. He handed it to Raphael. The mark had three sixes put together to make one symbol.

"It's worse than I thought," Raphael said.

"With this mark they are able to purchase things, even have health care. Those that don't have this mark, are considered traitors and they'll be arrested, or worse, killed," Gabriel said. "We cannot let that happen."

"We cannot stop what is to come," Raphael said. "God has made his choice. He will turn a blind eye to this nation and to the world. The war is coming, and when it does Christ will take back his kingdom." The other men agreed with a nod.

"When we get to the east, we will make the call," Victor said rising. He walked over to the horse to check over the weapons. Raphael rose and walked over to him.

"If there was a chance we could take back the power, we would do it," Raphael said. Victor smiled and shook his head.

"They have all turned their backs," he said placing several daggers in his coat.

"What about those who now worship God?" Raphael said.

"Then I hope they are able to continue worship without persecution. They will be the ones that will spread the gospel, without them…" Victor shook his head slowly. "Lucifer will reign through the people!" Raphael watched as Victor walked back over to the fire and sat down. Raphael returned to the fire and sat down on the log.

"How bad is it in Washington?" Gabriel asked.

"There's guards at every street corner, they keep a very good eye out. You can't escape from them. Some have been armed with horses," Raphael said.

"How did you escape?" Gabriel asked. Victor walked over and sat down beside him.

"Well we had received word that Damien had made an appearance and we rode up to Washington DC to see if we could stop him or at least slow him down but we got there too late. He had soldiers doing things that you couldn't even imagine," Raphael said. Victor looked over at him. "I mean gravesites were torn down, especially if a cross was on the tombstone, the American flags were burnt. There's no way to stop his agenda. People are beginning to side with him and he'll stop at nothing to make sure of that," he said. "By the end there will be nothing left, no peace, and no honor. He will strip everyone of their rights."

Gabriel listened as he ate a piece of meat. "There's no hope," he whispered. Victor looked over at him.

"There's always hope," he replied. "Don't forget that. That's why we're here." The men and Raphael looked over at Victor. Raphael frowned.

"We will take back our father's kingdom," he continued. "It will return to the way it once was." The men sat silently staring at the flames remembering back to the grace and beauty of how it was before. No fear, no sadness, just peace and beauty. It was something they had longed for, something they had treasured and wished for its return. "We rest tonight, we are safe here," Victor said, lying beside the log. He watched above him at the night sky through the tree branches. Gabriel laid down and soon fell asleep. Victor watched the others fall into a deep sleep then he slowly rose.

He walked down the trail and came to the opening and watched the star filled sky. The stars shined brightly in the darkness of the night. He smiled, seeing several deer run across the flat plains. He glanced up at the sky as he listened to the howling of the wolves in the distances. A flicker of light flashed across the midnight sky. Victor smiled, as a bright green wave moved across the sky. He looked back as another flash of light crossed from the north and another from the south. The wolves howled loudly all around him. Suddenly the lights lit up the sky coming from every direction and in every color. The lights slowly faded and everything became quiet. Smiling, Victor returned to the trail.

Morning crept by slowly. Victor rolled on his back as he remained asleep. Gabriel jerked awake and sat up. Glancing back he watched a lamb standing in the trail. Slowly he pushed the blanket back and rose. The lamb remained still as it stared at Gabriel.

It turned and made its way down the trail to a clearing. Gabriel came to the clearing and stopped as he looked down at the lamb. He glanced back hearing the rustling of the trees. A soft breeze blew through dense forest. Gabriel watched as a white horse and rider raced through the trees and into the opening. The man on the horse wore a crown and carried a sword. Gabriel watched the horse continue then disappear into the woods. Gabriel looked down at the lamb then back again. Another horse emerged from the woods across the opening. This time the body was red. The rider was carrying a sword, holding it in front of him as the horse charged across the field as if it was prepared for battle. Gabriel glanced back as a black horse charged into the opening, its rider carrying a balance in his hand as the horse stomped proudly through the open field. Gabriel looked down at the lamb. The lamb watched the horses cross, then disappear into the woods. Slowly a pale horse stumbled from the woods into the opening. Bones could be seen beneath its skin as it struggled to walk. The rider was thin and pale, his bones could be seen through his skin. Suddenly the sky became dark, the woods became black as night. The ground rumbled loudly as flashes could be seen all around. There was explosions as the sound of earthquakes rattled the woods. Men shouted as they raced across the open area with guns. Tanks moved across the field firing at everything around them. Gabriel gasped seeing huge explosions ripple through the sky. "No," he whispered seeing men and women fall across what had now become a battlefield. "No! Stop!" he screamed. A dark figure stood at the edge of the woods watching the war. He glanced over at Gabriel and smiled.

Gabriel jerked awake and sat up. Victor glanced over at him as he stomped out the fire. Gabriel glanced around slowly to see that they were still in the woods but morning had come and the thin mist had come in. The six men looked over at him. "You okay?" Victor asked. Gabriel glanced back at where the battle had taken place in his dream. He slowly rose and looked around the area. "Hey!" Victor said. Gabriel looked back at him.

"Yeah, yeah I'm fine," he said. Victor watched him in concern then continued putting out the fire.

"We'll be moving on today, we should be able to get to the east coast in two days," he said.

"This war…" Gabriel said. "It was different. Much different, there were no horses, but there were machines." Victor looked over at the other men then at Gabriel.

"They're called tanks," one of the men said.

"The point is, things have changed. There are weapons that we've never even thought of," Victor said. The other men agreed. Gabriel looked at the men then at Victor as he walked over to him. "Do not despair my brother, when the time has come we will meet at the battle field and the armies will come. We will stand by our brothers and we will march into battle," he said. Gabriel stood silently. Slowly he reached down and picked up his blanket from the ground. "I saw some berries not too far from here, I'm going to pick some so we'll have some food for the trip," Victor said. Gabriel nodded as Victor walked into the woods.

Victor walked through the dense forest and saw the berries on the bush. He quickly walked over and began to pick them and place them in a pouch. He could feel something watching him. He turned back and saw a branch shake as something flew from the tree. He grinned and went back to picking berries. Another branch rattled as Victor glanced over it. The branch shook as something else flew away from it. Victor watched the trees around him as he listened. Slowly he laid the pouch down and stepped away from the bush. Something flew through the woods and landed high in the tree. Victor watched the tree but didn't see anything. He stepped through the vines and watched ahead. Glancing up he saw an owl perched on a branch watching him. Victor smiled and walked back over to the bush and picked up the pouch of berries. Beginning to walk back to the camp he stopped feeling something watching from the branch close by. Glancing back he saw a shadow on the top branch of the tree. The animal stayed in the darkness as it watched him. "Hello?" Victor called, watching the bird like creature in the branches. The bird had a thin form, but its wings were capable of spreading up to ten feet. "Are you here to steal my food?" Victor called. The bird remained still. Victor laid out several berries on a leaf and moved back. He walked over to the log and knelt down behind it.

He could see the bird still perched on the branch watching. The bird flew down to the ground and landed beside the log. Victor saw a white eagle on the log pecking at the berries that he had left. He smiled seeing the eagle look over at him. It's piercing blue eyes watched him. Victor held out a berry as the eagle hopped down from the log and hopped over to Victor. It took the berry from his hand. Victor smiled. "Victor," Gabriel called from close by. Victor glanced back and rose. He looked back and saw that the eagle was now gone. He looked around the woods but the eagle was nowhere to be seen. Gabriel and the others walked over to Victor and stopped. "What's wrong?" he asked.

"The call has been made," Victor said glancing back at Gabriel.

"What do we do?" Gabriel asked as the others joined him.

"We go to the Middle East," Victor said.

Raphael nodded. "There are many people down in New Orleans that are in hiding. They're learning about God and praising him. They may not be warriors there, but they are in God's eyes." A howl pierced the air. They glanced back as shadows moved quickly through the dark woods. Smoke began to rise from the trees. "We have to move!" Raphael shouted as they raced over to the horses. Fire traveled violently through the trees.

They quickly climbed on their horses. Gabriel stared ahead as the wolf like creatures jumped unto the trail. Their long black fur was covered in ooze that dripped unto the ground like tar. Flames rose up from the area it soaked into.

"Gabe! Let's go!" Victor shouted holding out his hand. Gabriel stared at the creatures, watching as they slowly walked forward. Gabriel looked back at Victor knowing that he could hold them off long enough for them to get away. Victor shook his head. "No!" he shouted. Fire cut Gabriel off as the creatures surrounded him. Victor pulled his sword from the sheath and slid down from the saddle. He raced over to the fire as the flames rose to twice his size. Stopping, he watched helplessly as the creatures circled Gabriel.

"Get out of here!" Gabriel shouted. Victor stood motionless as Gabriel pulled out two daggers. "Go! Don't wait on me! I'll find you!" Gabriel shouted. Victor shook his head in anger as he raced back over to his horse and climbed into the saddle. The flames were now so high he couldn't see anything behind them. He quickly turned his horse as he followed the others through the woods. Gabriel turned back as the wolf like creatures watched him. One leapt at him. He slashed through it with his dagger. He knelt down with his daggers pointed in front of him, ready for the next one to attack. He was thrown to the ground as one of the creatures attacked him from behind. His daggers were thrown several feet away. The wolf like creature's claws dug deeply into his side. Gabriel struggled to grab his dagger but was cut off by the stabbing pain from the claws. Another wolf like creature grabbed his arm and yanked him back violently. There was the sound of wind coming through the trees. He gasped as he struggled to move away from the creatures that were now descending on him all together. Gabriel gasped in agony as he heard the loud roar of the wind. The trees swayed violently through the woods as a shadow passed through the branches. Gabriel gasped as he looked over at the creatures slowly backing away. Glancing back he watched as the white eagle swooped over the flames and flap his wings violently.

Smoke and flames engulfed the creatures as they moved back. Flames engulfed their black slick fur as they raced down the trail and into the woods. Gabriel gasped as he slowly rose. He held his side as he picked up his daggers. Looking over at the eagle he sighed as it watched it. "Thank you," he whispered. The eagle slowly turned its head sideways as if it was studying his wounds. "It's nothing, I'm fine," he whispered, struggling to step forward and keep his balance. He continued forward following along the path the others had taken.

Victor and the others rode towards the mountain ranges of the east known at the Appalachian Mountains. Pulling his horse to a stop, Victor glanced back. They were so far ahead now that turning back to see if they could find Gabriel would take hours. Raphael rode up beside him. "We have to continue on," he said.

"No, we need to rest," Victor sighed.

"But sir…!" Raphael began.

"I said no!" Victor snapped, looking back at him.

Raphael knew Victor wanted to give Gabriel a chance to catch up if he was able to. "We'll rest here tonight," he said seeing a cave ahead of them. They rode their horses to the entrance of the cave.

"I'll get a fire started," Raphael said sliding down from the saddle and entering the cave. Victor slid down from the saddle and watched the woods around them. There were no sounds or any movement. He feared for Gabriel's safety, but he knew that Gabriel would be protected by God. Their father would not let any harm come to them. He walked away and entered the inside of the cave.

CHAPTER SEVEN

Raphael sat beside the fire warming his hands as night had fallen over the mountain range. He glanced over at Victor who was keeping an eye on the entrance of the cave. "He'll catch up," Raphael said as two of the men returned with several rabbits and a bird.

As the night continued, Victor pulled off several pieces of meat from the rabbit. He looked over at the entrance of the cave and sighed heavily. The other men could tell that he was concerned. "He's tough. He'll meet back up with us," one of the men said offering some hope. Victor continued to watch the entrance of the cave waiting for any signs of Gabriel or even the white eagle.

Morning came as Victor laid asleep beside the fire. He woke to the crackling of the wood. Sitting up he wiped the sleep from his eyes as he looked around the cave. Raphael was still sitting and watching the entrance on alert at any signs of someone coming. "How long have I been asleep?" Victor asked.

"Since last night," Raphael said. Victor watched the entrance of the cave.

"Any signs of him?" Victor asked. Raphael shook his head.

"Just a couple rabbits and some birds, nothing else," he said. The sounds of rocks falling outside the cave alerted them. The others woke quickly and moved back away from the entrance. Victor and Raphael rose and pulled out their swords prepared for someone to enter. Victor watched several rocks fall and land in front of the cave, a twig with leaves and some berries landed beside the rocks. The swooshing sound of wings could be heard. Victor raced to the entrance of the cave and quickly hurried outside. He glanced back as the eagle disappeared into the woods. Looking down at the items laid before his feet, he knelt down and picked them up. Raphael walked over and looked at them. There was something about the items that the eagle had brought, something that could make a medicine or possibly even a spell to draw a demon out of hiding.

Victor walked down the trail and looked around. He stopped, seeing the eagle sitting on a branch watching him. The eagle swooped down and landed on his stretched out arm. The screech of the eagle caused the land to vibrate. Victor closed his eyes as the breeze brushed his face.

The calmness took him away from the pain and torture of the world. He glanced forward and found himself on the trail outside the gates of Heaven. He walked down the trail and stopped, seeing a guard standing silently. The guard saluted him as he walked by. Victor stopped, seeing a man dressed in white before him. He walked forward and knelt in front of the man. With a smile, the man walked towards him. "Michael, you have been missed," he said. Victor smiled.

"Christ, I bow before you," he said, kneeling.

"Rise," Christ said as Victor rose slowly. "Your job is not complete as of yet."

"What must I do?" Victor asked, walking with Christ down the trail.

"There will be a turning point where no man or woman will stop this downfall," Christ said.

"But we must stop this destruction, this torture of mankind," Victor said, stopping and looking at him.

"I'm afraid there is no turning back now," Christ replied. Victor fell silent. "Without knowing the one true Lord, their torture will not end," Christ said. "This war will go on until no man stands."

"What about those who fought in those battles?" Victor said.

"They have seen victories, they know the true meaning of battle, they have fought for what they stand for," Christ said. "Much like you and your army."

"Does this world stand for nothing?" Victor snapped. "Do they not see what is before their eyes?"

"No, they are blinded by their greed and their lies," Christ said. "That is where you will come in, you will lead them. Lead them to see what their eyes cannot."

"I have to find my brother," Victor said. "I cannot do this without him," Victor said. Christ stared at him.

"Do not worry, he will find you. You will lead this war, thousands upon thousands will follow you," Christ said. "You will no longer be known as Victor, for that is a human name, not the name of a warrior. You will be known as Michael from here on out," he said. Michael nodded slowly as Christ walked over to him and smiled. "You know your place," Christ said. Michael nodded slowly. "Gabriel will come to you, but do not be deceived, for Satan will try and confuse you," Christ said. "Fear not for his safety." Michael slowly walked away. "I will see you as the sun rises on the first day of the eighth year," Christ called.

Victor, now known as Michael gasped as he opened his eyes. He looked around and saw that the eagle was now gone. Glancing forward, he saw Gabriel standing on the trail staring at him. "Gabriel," he said, rising.

Gabriel's clothes were covered in blood. Michael raced over to him.

"The eagle led me here," he said.

"It is good to see you my brother," Michael smiled.

"Good to see you too brother," Gabriel said with a nod. He looked down at the blood on his hands.

"You're injured," Michael said.

"Nothing but a scratch," Gabriel replied. Michael forced him to turn. He winced seeing the deep gashes going down his side. Michael helped him towards the cave they had taken cover in. Michael helped him into the cave. The other men looked over at them.

"You talked with him Michael?" Raphael asked rising.

"I did," Michael said with a nod. Gabriel glanced over at Michael. "We will move on tomorrow. It will give us a chance to get collected here over night."

"But we must move on now, we need to make it to Washington," Gabriel said.

"No, you're not riding into the city with those injuries. They will see this and they will have your head," Michael said.

"My head?" Gabriel asked.

"Christians are being killed," Raphael said as Gabriel looked at him. "They see that you are injured they'll assume you've escaped somehow and they will take you in as prisoner. They have already started this in our town. Teenagers are slaughtered and for what?

For reading the Bible, for wearing a cross necklace. This country is no longer free but taken over by those that wish it to be destroyed," Raphael said. Michael walked over and took the bowl and plants that the eagle had delivered. Gabriel sat down slowly in front of Michael and removed his shirt. He cringed in agony as he laid his shirt down. Michael stared at the deep wounds on Gabriel's back. Raphael stared at the wounds. He shook his head slowly. "He's in for a rough night."

"I dare not close my eyes, my nightmares will take the best of me," Gabriel said. Michael crushed the plants against the rocks to make a paste. He slowly covered the wounds with the paste and laid a leaf across it for a dressing. Gabriel cringed in agony. The other men watched the flames of the fire, they had no fear or any signs of being restless in their eyes. They were calm and still as if they were listening to a message. Michael slowly placed a shawl over Gabriel's shoulders as they sat close to the fire.

As evening came Gabriel laid close to the fire, still not tired but the feeling of weakness had overwhelmed him. He watched Michael stand at the entrance of the cave. Raphael took a sip of warm tea from a small cup as he watched Gabriel. Michael continued to watch the rain fall outside of the cave. Raphael rose and walked over to Michael. "You are worried brother?" Raphael asked. He handed a small cup of tea to Michael.

Michael took it and swallowed it. He handed the cup to Raphael.

"Not worried," Michael said.

"You have changed since you've talked to him," Raphael said.

"There is something different about my brother," Michael said. Raphael looked over at Gabriel still lying awake beside the fire.

"You do not trust him?" Raphael asked. Michael stared forward.

"I was warned not to let him deceive me," he said. Raphael grinned.

Gabriel shook his head. "I would never!" he said. Michael moved from the entrance of the cave. Raphael watched a shadow move slowly through the rain. He grinned as he glanced back at Gabriel. Gabriel stared at Michael as he walked over and knelt down.

"You know, those dogs would've done a lot more damage than what they did knowing that you're an angel," he said. Gabriel grinned.

"What?" he said.

"You had a long walk for being hurt so bad," Michael said reaching out to touch him. Raphael walked over as the others rose, ready to draw their swords. Gabriel backed away. "What's wrong?" Michael said motioning for the men to take him. They grabbed Gabriel's arms and yanked him up. Gabriel screamed in agony.

"No, stop!" he screamed as Michael walked up to him. Gabriel yelled and struggled against the men. Michael wiped his finger down Gabriel's forehead and between his eyes. Dirt and mud slowly wiped away from an upside down cross. Gabriel smiled and laughed.

"You guys are smart!" He said in a deep growl. He yanked away from the men violently and climbed up on the rocks. "My master will not fall, as hard as you try you cannot defeat him!" he snapped, hissing at several of the men.

"Where is my brother?" Michael asked drawing his sword and holding out to the demon that had taken on Gabriel's appearance. Gabriel laughed as he bounced from rock to rock like a wild animal.

"Don't worry, he's safe…for now!" Gabriel snapped. Several of the men threw a rope around Gabriel's neck and slid him down from the rock. They pulled him over and held him in place as Michael pressed the sword against his neck.

"I will ask again, where is my brother?" Michael asked.

"At the feet of my master," Gabriel snapped. Michael forced his sword through the stomach of the demon. The men allowed the body to fall to the ground.

"How did you know?" Raphael asked. Michael slid his sword into the sheath.

"My brother would've waited for the cover of darkness and sneak through the stillness of the night, unnoticed," he said. The sound of movement outside alerted them. Michael drew his sword and moved quickly but quietly to the side of the cave. Movement could be heard coming up next to the cave entrance. Michael listened to the movement, which was light but quick. Raphael watched silently with a dagger in his hand. The wind blew violently outside as rain continued to come down. There was a faint whistle. Raphael whistled back a response. Another whistle could be heard. Raphael lowered his daggers as he raced from the cave. Michael lowered his sword to the sound of movement. Raphael returned with the real Gabriel that had been attacked in the woods. "Gabe!" Michael said, rushing over to him. Blood covered his body from the gruesome attack. He collapsed as Michael grabbed hold of him and helped him to the ground. Raphael knelt down beside him.

"I told you….not to wait!" Gabriel whispered. His body was soaked from the rain and his blood.

"How did you get away?" Michael asked brushing his wet hair from his face.

"I prayed," Gabriel whispered.

"They're coming." Raphael said as he watched Gabriel. He shook his head. "We can't ride with him like this," he said.

"You…have to," Gabriel said. "You have to go, the people are in danger….please!"

"People of the city would have things to help, right?" Michael asked.

"I...I don't know," Raphael said. "There's rumors of two guardian angels."

"Jared and Anastasia, yes, I know them," Michael said with a nod. "Where are they now?"

"Washington DC, waiting for your arrival," Raphael said. "There's also rumors of two witnesses there."

Michael nodded. "We ride overnight," he said, wrapping his brother's arm around his neck and helping him rise. They quickly hurried from the cave. The men looked down at the demon.

"What about him?" one of the men asked.

"Get rid of it," Raphael said, quickly leaving the cave as the men gathered their gear and turned back to the body.

The sun slowly rose in the distance as the mountains remained under a shade of dark cloud cover. The horses continued along a path across the flat land leading towards the city. Michael held steady as his brother sat sideways across the saddle in front of him, leaning against him. He could feel the weak breaths against his neck. His skin was hot, the attack had poisoned his body with sin. There was no way to stop the attack that had overwhelmed him. Michael pulled the horse to a stop seeing the city ahead. He glanced over at Raphael and the others. "Go around and meet up with us under the cover of darkness," Michael said.

Raphael nodded and rode with the others around the city. Gabriel groaned and looked over at the city.

"Where are we?" he whispered too weak to lift his head.

"Washington DC," Michael said. Gabriel cringed and rested his head back down on Michael's shoulder, he didn't want to see the city nor be there. "I agree," Michael said knowing the frustration of having to enter this city. He continued forcing the horse forward.

The horse slowly stepped down the trail. Each step caused a weak groan to come from Gabriel. The ride was becoming increasingly more and more uncomfortable for Gabriel, to the point where he was clutching Michael's shirt in agony, begging to stop. The horse stopped as they came to a small house. Michael forced Gabriel to sit forward. "Sit here for a minute," he said sliding down from the horse. Gabriel stared at the house and then looked around the woods keeping a close eye to see if someone was watching from the woods. Michael returned from the house. "We're safe here," he said. He helped Gabriel down from the horse.

The fire crackled softly in the fireplace as Gabriel laid on his stomach on the bed. His shirt was off, deep gashes covered his body from his neck to his waist. Strips of wet cloth covered the wounds. Michael returned to the house with a basket of herbs and plants. He sat them down on the table and walked over to the bed. He slowly felt Gabriel's forehead and frowned, feeling that the fever had risen more. He glanced over at Jared and Anastasia entered. "I thought someone had come," Anastasia said. Michael rose as he looked at her then down at Gabriel. "What happened?" Anastasia asked racing over.

"He was attacked in the woods," Michael said. Anastasia moved the blankets back slowly.

"By hounds?" she asked.

"Yeah," Michael said with a nod. Jared felt his forehead and checked his breathing.

"He's very weak. He's being tormented by the fever," he said.

"I found some herbs to reduce it," Michael said. Anastasia raced over to table. She quickly filled the cup with a small amount of water and grinded the herbs into it. She handed the cup to Jared. Jared sat down beside Gabriel. Slowly he took a small amount and streaked it across Gabriel's forehead. Anastasia walked back to the fireplace and slowly stirred some herbs into the water that was boiling in a pot over the fire. "So we're going old school?" Michael asked. Anastasia glanced back at him.

"You obviously don't know about the government," she said.

"I was a police officer, I know about the government," Michael replied.

"We use electricity they charge us, they charge us then they'll find us, if we're found we get caught, end of story," Anastasia said.

"She's right, we can't risk it," Jared said.

"And at night?" Michael asked.

"Candles," Jared said.

"Old school," Anastasia said. Michael smiled. Anastasia slowly poured some herbs blended with water into a cup. Gabriel rolled on his back as Jared lifted his head to the cup. Gabriel cringed as he sipped some of the water. Jared rested his head back down on the pillow.

"How long does this take to work?" Michael asked. Gabriel cringed in agony as he moaned. "That was quick," Michael said. Gabriel groaned and rolled on his side. Anastasia sat beside him and pressed a wash cloth on his forehead. "Where are the weapons?" Michael asked.

"Back room," Jared said. Michael nodded and hurried to the back room.

Michael pulled several swords from the bag and checked each one for damage. Jared entered the room and shut the door. "The city is bad," he said. "I mean we watched a woman be told that if she didn't receive the mark she would killed," he said. Michael looked over at him.

"Did she?" he asked.

"No, no she didn't receive the mark," Jared said. Michael looked back down at the bag. "People are being slaughtered. The cops are against their own people," Jared said shaking his head. "I fear for them."

Michael nodded as he placed the weapons back in the bag.

"It'll only get worse," he said. Jared nodded.

"What did you see?" he asked.

"Camps are set up, people are being tortured," Michael said grabbing the second bag. "But I did see hope," he said looking over at Jared. "The white eagle."

"You saw the white eagle?" Jared asked.

"I did," Michael said with a nod. Jared smiled.

"That's wonderful news," he said.

"Tomorrow I'm going to travel into the city," Michael said. "Do you care to join me?"

"If I must," Jared said. Michael nodded. The sound of horses coming closer alerted them. They quickly returned to the room as Raphael and the others entered. Anastasia rose as Michael and Jared came into the room.

"Most of the streets are blocked off," Raphael said as his men entered the cabin and shut the door. "We can't get into the city," he continued.

"We'll get in one way or another," Michael said.

"If they find out about us being there we will be put into camps and tortured," Raphael said.

"My Father is stronger than them," Michael said. Raphael nodded. Raphael and the others laid their coats down on the bench beside the door. They walked over to the fire and warmed their hands. Michael slowly sat down in a chair close by and watched Anastasia still working on Gabriel's wounds.

As night came the temperature drastically dropped. Anastasia slowly pressed the covers down over Gabriel. Michael wrapped a blanket around his arms. Anastasia looked over at the window to the sound of screams of horror and pain. Michael was already on his feet and walking towards the door. He slowly stepped outside as more screams could be heard followed by cheering from the middle of the city. Michael could see fire and flames rising as the cheering continued. "Raphael join me, you guys stay here," Michael said as they started forward. The others returned to the house.

Entering the city, the cheering was getting louder and louder as they walked towards the middle of the city. Raphael and Michael stopped at the corner of the one of the buildings and saw thousands of people surrounding a platform. There were five people on the platform with nooses around their necks. People cheered loudly and shouted profanity at them. Several threw stones, striking them in the face. An officer walked up unto the platform and motioned for everyone to quiet down. The crowd fell silent as the officer began talking. "We will not let our country be overrun by these people," he called. The crowd cheered loudly. The officer held up the Bible as the crowd grew angry. "They were caught reading this to each other!" the officer shouted. "We will not allow this!" Michael and Raphael looked at each other. They glanced back as several officers walked unto the platform. "Their punishment for this is death!" the officer called. He tossed the Bible into a trashcan that was on fire. Michael stared ahead in anger as the officer walked from the platform. The officer pulled the lever and the five people dropped down. They hung lifelessly from the ropes. Raphael turned away as Michael watched in disbelief.

"Come, we need to get back," Michael said walking away. Raphael quickly followed.

Anastasia sat beside the fire rubbing her hands together. She sighed heavily as she waited for Michael and Raphael to return. She glanced over her shoulder at Gabriel who was tucked under several blankets. She remembered the young child she was to watch over, it was her job to keep her safe. She missed the innocence of the children that she would see on the playground. The child had died young to a form of cancer. The pain the child had gone through was hard to watch, but watching the child play in the grass fields of Heaven and dance along the trails made all the sadness go away. Slowly Anastasia rose and walked over to Gabriel. Sitting down beside him she slowly slid her hand down his cheek. The fever had broken. Slowly she climbed over to the empty side of the bed and laid down beside him. Soon she had drifted into a deep sleep.

Michael and Raphael returned to the small house and stopped seeing the two asleep. Michael smiled and walked over to the fireplace. The air in the house was warm compared to the chilled air outside. He slowly pulled up a chair and sat down. Raphael pulled up a chair beside him and sat down. "This won't last forever," he said. Michael frowned as he stared at the fire.

"I know," he said. Raphael turned back as the men rode in on their horses. He rose and walked over to the door. The men entered the house.

"The area is clear," one of the men said.

"But we're safe here! I mean we could just stay," Raphael said. Michael shook his head.

"The war will be in the middle east, we must go," he said.

"But what about God's people here?" one of the men asked.

"I know we want to protect them but…we have a job to do," Michael said. Anastasia lay awake listening. She knew that Michael had to follow commands. It wasn't his place to question them. The sound of crackling wood in the fireplace drowned out the conversation taking place in the next room. Slowly she drifted off to sleep as the night continued.

In the morning a chill came in through the window. The fire in the fireplace was still burning. Anastasia woke slowly and saw that Gabriel was no longer beside her. She sat up and glanced around the cabin. It was empty. She wondered if they had left without even a good bye, but she knew that they would never do that. She saw the weapons still nestled under the table. She looked over at the end table and saw her bow and arrow still there. Looking at her wrist she smiled seeing a bracelet made out leaves neatly braided together. She glanced out the window to the sound of a whistle. Rising quickly she made her way to the door and outside.

Gabriel was filling the canisters with water from the stream behind the house. Michael was sitting beside the post carving a whistle from a piece of wood. He glanced over at her and smiled. "Good morning," he said.

"Morning," Anastasia said. Gabriel walked over and sat down on the log close by. He handed one of the canisters to Michael. Michael nodded and took it. Gabriel was now wearing a black vest over his bare chest and jeans. His muscles seemed to have grown over night and his short blondish brown hair made his blue eyes sparkle more. "Thanks," Anastasia said holding up her wrist showing him the bracelet.

"You're welcome," Gabriel grinned.

"Where are the others?" Anastasia asked.

"In town to get supplies," Michael said. Anastasia glanced around slowly and looked over at the trail.

"How long have they been gone?" she asked. "About an hour. Why?" Michael asked. Anastasia listened to the birds sitting in the trees then looked at the trail. "Speak!" Michael said rising. Anastasia looked back at him.

"Something's not right," she said. Gabriel rose and listened. "The birds, they're silent. Raphael and his men won't return to this spot if there is trouble. They won't give up their leader," she continued. Michael and Gabriel quickly hurried to the house. Michael forced Gabriel inside as Anastasia stood silently looking down the trail. Beyond the trees on the outside of the woods she could see a police car coming down the road. Quickly she hurried back inside.

Michael followed her in. "Get the fire out," he called. Gabriel dumped the water on the fire and quickly got down behind the bed as Anastasia got down beside him. Michael hid beside the dresser closer to the window. He watched as the cop car pulled to a stop and an officer step out. Michael looked at the others and motioned them to keep silent. He gripped the sword beside him as Anastasia clutched the bow and arrow in her hands. Gabriel held the dagger tightly as he listened. The sound of footsteps could be heard outside. Gabriel looked through the crack in the boards beneath the window and watched.

The officer walked over to where Michael had been sitting, creating a whistle. He slowly slid his fingers through the small pieces of wood that had been cut off the whistle. He slowly walked over to the fence where the horses had been tied. He knelt down and looked at the hoof prints in the mud. Another officer joined him. "Someone's been here," the officer said to the other one. The other officer walked over to the door and knocked on it. Gabriel and Anastasia sat back against the bed frame. There was another knock. Gabriel looked over at Michael. Michael shook his head slowly, motioning them to keep quiet rather than risk the chance of answering the door. He watched the door handle rattle as the officers attempted to enter but it was locked. Michael prayed that they wouldn't attempt to open it and force their way in. Gabriel and Anastasia glanced back as the officers walked around the house, slowly glancing in through the windows. Gabriel moved against the wall beside Anastasia, they waited in fear as the officer continued around the house. More talking could be heard as several officers joined them. The back door handle rattled. "Ram the door," the officer said. Anastasia gripped her bow and arrow and looked at Gabriel.

"No!" Gabriel whispered.

"Go!" Anastasia said. "Please! I'll hold them off!" She slid the bags over to Gabriel. Gabriel took the bags slowly as Anastasia handed him the bracelet. "Hold on to it for me," she said. Gabriel rose and took the bags as Michael raced over. They quickly ran out the side door and hid in the woods. Anastasia rose as the doors in the front and back could be heard being kicked open. Anastasia watched as the officers entered the cabin.

"Well...look what we have here," the leader officer said with a smile. She clutched the bow and arrow at her side. The officers stop as they surrounded her. "She's armed." Anastasia smiled.

"It's not me you have to worry about," she said. The officers looked around the cabin.

"You're the only one here my dear," said another officer. Anastasia smiled.

"Is that so?" she asked. The officers looked at one another as they tried to decide what to do next. Suddenly the floor began to vibrate, like the sound of a stampede coming through the woods. Listening, Anastasia smiled as she looked at the officers.

"What is that?" one of the officers asked as the building shook violently. The windows shattered as the officers got down and covered their heads. They quickly rose and raced outside. "Get to the car!" they shouted at one another as they raced back to the road. She sighed and walked out the front door and glanced over. Jared sat on the horse with a smile.

"Nice sound effects," Anastasia said placing the bow and arrow over her shoulder.

"I couldn't resist," Jared said. Anastasia smiled and walked over to the horse. Jared took her hand and pulled her on the horse behind him. They rode slowly down the trail away from the cabin.

Anastasia watched ahead as they rode down a road leading to a half torn down church. "What is this place?" she asked.

"A place of meeting," Jared said. Anastasia smiled, seeing the other horses and the car out front. The door to the run down church opened as Gabriel raced outside. Sliding down from the horse, Anastasia raced over to him. He pulled her into a hug and turned her in a circle.

"You alright?" Anastasia asked. Gabriel smiled and nodded.

"You?" he asked.

"You know I am," Anastasia said.

"What? No hug for me?" Jared said sliding down from the saddle. Anastasia smiled as she looked over at Jared. Jared placed his arm around Gabriel as they walked toward the church. Anastasia looked up at the building and at the gardens around it. Everything was run down and decaying. It was the last place anyone would look for people because it didn't provide much cover because some of the boards were missing and windows were blown out.

They entered the church and shut the door. Anastasia walked over to the long staircase and looked up at the second floor. She walked up the steps as she slid her hand along the railing. She stopped half way and looked around the church. She stepped back down the steps as the other angels stood silently. "It's beautiful," she said. They looked at her.

"It's an old, run down church," one of the men said.

"No! Just remember what it once was," Anastasia said. She walked over to the wall. "The wall here…it had a desk in front of it that held the offering plates, ones made of gold!"

Gabriel smiled. "Over here…" Anastasia said walking over to the doors. "There were stained glass windows looking in at the auditorium," she said. Michael smiled as he began to see it. Anastasia opened the doors and entered the worship area. The others entered behind her. The seat cushions are missing from the benches. The Church had stripped of the cross, the altar and the seats. Anastasia's smile faded. It was nothing but a skeleton. Gabriel walked over to her.

"What about here?" Gabriel asked. Anastasia stared at the room. She walked to the front and walked past where once the altar stood. She slowly knelt down and wiped her fingers across the dried blood on the floor.

"They took shelter here," she said softly, "but they were followed." Gabriel looked back at Michael then at Anastasia. "They locked the doors but that didn't keep them out," Anastasia said. "The hate! The sin!" she continued. "It came in and stripped the people of their rights. Where did the world go so wrong?" she asked. Gabriel walked over to her.

"They took shelter here because it was one place they could go where they felt it was their home," he said. Michael nodded. "It's our home!" Gabriel said. Anastasia nodded. "You see, they take away the rights of the people, they take away the Bibles, they take away the churches but they cannot take away their God. He still strives here. This is God's house. No matter how run down it is, no matter how bare the bones are, he is here and here he will stay," he said. "We will rebuild it and when they come, we will offer them hope." Anastasia smiled and nodded.

"And we will help them learn about their true King," Michael said.

"No matter what, they will always be welcomed here," Raphael said. The others nodded.

"First order of business, we need to place the weapons in a safe place, out of sight if anyone stops by," Michael said handing one of the men the bags of weapons.

"Upstairs, room on the left, there's a panic room," Raphael said.

"A church with a panic room?" Anastasia asked.

"It was built recently, those that took shelter here must have known what was coming," Raphael said. Two of the angels walked up from the room and up the steps to the second floor.

On the second floor Anastasia entered a room and stopped. Glancing around, she saw a bed and dresser and closet. She smiled knowing that a woman had once lived in the room. The bedspread had a floral print and the curtains were a beautiful white color. She walked over to the closet and slowly opened the wooden doors. Smiling, she slowly pulled out a white silk gown. Walking over to the mirror she smiled as she held it up to her body as she admired herself. The sound of chirping came through the opened window. She smiled and laid the dress on the bed and opened the curtains. A garden took over most of the land behind the church. She quickly hurried from the room.

Slowly she entered the garden and looked around. The stone walk way was almost completely stripped away. She stopped, seeing Gabriel standing near the old fountain that no longer worked. He stood listening with his eyes shut. He now wore a peasant top, black pants and black riding boots. Anastasia walked over to him and stood beside him. "It's beautiful," she said. Gabriel smiled and nodded.

"It is," he said. They stood silently as they admired the garden. Anastasia walked over to the water fountain.

"Is it like the Garden of Eden?" she asked.

"It's the same," Gabriel said looking at her. Anastasia smiled. "It's the way it should've been," Gabriel said. Anastasia walked over to a rose bush and stopped. She looked between the thorn branches and reached in. Gabriel walked over as she pulled out a white rose.

"There is still beauty within," Gabriel said. Anastasia slowly handed him the rose and walked from the garden. Gabriel looked down at the rose then at the garden. He looked over at the rose bush and saw that there were now at least a dozen roses on the bush. Smiling, Gabriel walked slowly through the garden. There were many different trees that were dead and decayed. He stopped at a tree and stared at it. Glancing over he saw a white marble bench sitting beneath it. Walking over he sat down and observed the garden around him. Michael walked over and sat down beside him.

"Remind you of home?" he asked.

"Just a little," Gabriel said. "It needs work." Michael glanced forward at the tree.

"We're safe here," he said.

"Those in the city are not," Gabriel said. "Is it our job to help them?"

"That's always been our job," Michael said. "I mean we can't sit here and do nothing, I'll be heading into the city in the morning to see just how bad it really is," he said.

"Do you really want to know?" Gabriel asked.

"No, not really, but I have to. I have to know what we're against," Michael said. Gabriel sighed as Michael patted his shoulder and walked back to the building.

That night Anastasia sat on the bed, watching the night sky that was in full view from the window. Rising, she walked over to the window and sat down on the window seal. She stared up at the stars as rumbling could be heard in the distances. Rising, she watched as lights moved across the sky. Quickly, she raced from the room and down the steps. "What is that?" one of the men called as everyone raced down the hall.

They hurried outside and stopped, seeing helicopters by the thousands flying across the sky. "What are they doing?" Gabriel asked looking at Michael.

"They're moving east," Michael said. "They're preparing for war." They continued to watch the helicopters move across the night sky.

"There's no way to fight this. They have machines!" Raphael called.

"They have machines but they are no match for God," Michael said. "We head into the city in the morning," he said, returning to the building. Anastasia watched as the helicopters slowly vanished into the night sky and everything became silent again.

CHAPTER EIGHT

Michael walked down the city street with Gabriel and Raphael. Many stores had shut down and those that were still open had signs posted for new Christians to stay out or face death. Michael, Raphael and Gabriel entered one of the stores. The store was run down and most of the shelves were empty. Gabriel walked over to the shelf and picked up a package of doughnuts. "Hey Mike!" he called. Michael grinned and looked back at him.

"Mike?" he said.

"Doughnuts?" Gabriel asked. "I mean you were a police officer." Michael frowned as Gabriel flashed a smile showing his dimples. Michael shook his head.

"Fine," he said, knowing he did have a craving for doughnuts. Raphael walked over to the shelf and grabbed a stack of twelve waters. He stopped seeing an upside down cross on the wall behind the checkout counter. He glanced over at Michael who had spotted it at the same time.

The man walked over to the register. "Can I help you?" he asked acting like he had been working for a while and was not interested in helping another customer. Gabriel handed him the package of doughnuts and waters. "I need your bar code to scan," the man said.

"Bar code?" Gabriel asked.

"Your chip, in your wrist," the man said.

"Um…" Gabriel whispered, not knowing what to do.

"No bar code, no buying," the man said. "It's the law!" Michael walked over to the counter.

"I know the law," he whispered in a deep voice. The man at the counter stared at him. "The kid wants to check out, I think you should ring those items up for him," he said. The man stared at Michael in fear. He nodded and quickly began to scan the items. Michael patted Gabriel shoulder as he walked past him over to the window. He watched outside as the man finished the order. The man handed the bag to Gabriel.

"Thank you," Gabriel said, taking the bag and walked out the door. They walked down the street and stopped to the sounds of screams. Michael and Raphael listened to the cheering from the center of the city. Michael walked over to Gabriel.

"Get that stuff home!" he said. Gabriel nodded and hurried down the alley. Michael and Raphael walked towards the city center and stopped, seeing people being led down the street as people shouted and threw rocks at them. Raphael stepped forward but was pulled back by Michael. "We step in to help brother, what would be our fate?" Michael asked. Raphael stepped back slowly as he watched the people being led to a platform. The women of the group were screaming and crying, knowing their fate. Michael and Raphael watched. He could feel someone staring at them. Glancing back he could see Damien overseeing the event from the White House balcony. "We got to go," Michael said quickly hurrying down the alley with Raphael. They stopped when they saw several cops blocking the alley. They quickly raced into the nearest building.

Raphael stopped and shut the door. He watched the officers look around slowly then continued down the alley. Michael gazed at them and listened. There are several sniffles from the darkness of the room. Moving away from the door, Michael could see several families observing him. The teens were terrified as the parents hugged them tightly. Michael could see Bibles hidden beneath the table. "It's alright," he said stepping forward.

"You're a police officer?" one of the fathers asked, seeing the police uniform.

"I was before the rapture," Michael said.

"He's an angel," one of the girls said. Michael smiled and knelt down slowly as the girl watched him.

"How do you know?" Michael asked.

"Because I can see your wings," she said. Michael smiled. "He's one too," the girl said looking at Raphael.

"Angels?" one of the mothers asked. She quickly pulled her back.

"We are staying at a church on the outside of the city," Michael said. The families looked at one another not knowing whether or not to trust the two men.

"Can we go Mom?" One of the girls asked. "It's scary here."

"It'll only get worse in the city," Michael said. "It's no place for your families." The families continued to stare at each other, knowing deep in their hearts they wanted to follow.

At the run down church Anastasia laid in the grass wearing the white gown. She smiled as she held a piece of grass between her teeth. A small rabbit came up to her and nibbled the grass from her mouth. Anastasia smiled as the bunny ate the rest of the sliver of grass. She glanced back as Gabriel came from the building and walked over to her. He laid down in the grass next to her. "You're worried," Anastasia observed. Gabriel looked over at her.

"It was worse than I thought," he said.

"How did you think it was going to be?" Anastasia asked. He placed his hands behind his head and rested his head back on them. Anastasia laid her head down on his arm and looked at him. "Do not despair," she said. "God will win."

"I know," Gabriel responded. Anastasia smiled as Gabriel wrapped his arm around her. "The sky has lost its beauty," Gabriel said, seeing that the sky was no longer blue but a slight shade of gray.

"It's only resting, resting for when Christ returns," Anastasia said. Gabriel smiled and nodded. "Come! I have to show you something," Anastasia said, rising. Gabriel rose and followed her down the path to the garden. "Shut your eyes," Anastasia said. Gabriel nodded and shut his eyes as Anastasia opened the gate and led him into the garden. "Okay, open them," she commanded. Gabriel opened his eyes and looked around. The garden had been cleaned, all the vines over the walkway had been cleared away.

"This looks great," Gabriel said. Anastasia smiled.

"When the time comes, the flowers will bloom and the trees will come alive!" she smiled.

"And there will be enough fruit to feed many," Gabriel said. Anastasia laughed and nodded. They glanced back at the sound of a car arriving. Gabriel and Anastasia quickly hurried from the garden, shutting the gate behind them. They raced to the driveway and stopped, seeing two families standing alongside Michael and Raphael.

Several of the men led the families inside. "Are we taking in homeless now?" Gabriel asked.

"They're Christians," Michael said walking towards the door. Gabriel grabbed his arm.

"And what if they are not? They might give us away to the enemy," he frowned. Michael stared at him then yanked his arm away.

"This isn't up for discussion," Michael said, walking into the house. Gabriel looked over at Raphael.

"He's right, they had taken shelter in an abandoned building in town," Raphael said. Quickly he walked past them and entered the building.

In the stable, Gabriel slowly brushed the horse's side. He walked to the front of the horse. "Lucky you, you don't have to deal with this," he said with a smile. He walked around the horse. He combed the horse's mane. He glanced over as Anastasia appeared at the entrance to the barn. "Horses are lucky, all they have to worry about is what part of the pasture to eat from. Unlike us having to worry about where we are going next, where the war will be," he said.

"Are you traveling with them?" Anastasia asked.

"What choice do I have?" Gabriel asked. "There's a war coming, but you wouldn't understand, you're not a warrior," he added, laying the brush down.

"But I am!" Anastasia snapped. "I have fought much more than you or any warrior angel." Gabriel grabbed the next brush from the box.

"War is no place for a guardian angel," he said.

"Neither is it a place for a messenger," Anastasia argued. Gabriel looked over at her as he stopped brushing the horse. "You may be part of the royal line known as the archangels but that will not stop the enemy."

"Why are you here?" Gabriel asked, looking at her. "I do not need protecting." Anastasia stared at him knowing that angels were not meant to love, but to only love as family. "I love my family, I do," Gabriel said. "I will not have a say in who goes to war and who doesn't. My brother is my leader, I will follow him to battle if it is his will," he said.

"And when Damien comes and strikes down those soldiers that fight on our side what then? Will you step in front of them and take the wrath of the blade? Or will you stand by and watch?" Anastasia snapped. "I see it in your eyes, you care about those people, that's what makes you strong. Will you bear their pain and take it upon yourself? Will you allow them to run while you fight?" Gabriel turned back to the horse. "Will you allow that serpent to return and steal away from what God, our father, had given you to protect? To keep out?"

"I am a warrior, if Michael wants me at his side then I will follow my brother into war! If I'm to fall at the blade, I will do so with honor," Gabriel snapped back.

"Then you have chosen your path, I hope you see it well," Anastasia frowned walking from the barn. Gabriel groaned.

"I bet ladies don't treat you like that," he said, looking at the horse with a smile.

Anastasia sat on the floor beside the children that were between the ages of twelve and fourteen. She smiled watching them play a game. She glanced over as one of Raphael's men entered the house. Michael and Raphael walked over and listened to the man talking. They quickly raced outside. She quickly rose and followed as Gabriel rode up to the building on the horse. Michael raced over to him as Gabriel slid down from the saddle. "Were you seen?" he asked.

"No, but the cops have taken to the streets. The Christians who are in hiding risk the chance of being found. Cops are going into every building, searching it from ceiling to floor, and once they are done they burn it," Gabriel said. "Damien gave the order that if any Christians are found they are to be put in prison." Michael looked over at Raphael then at Gabriel. "Those that do come out willingly...they keep the men and the older boys. They take the women and children and threaten the men, that if they don't fight in this war they will kill the women and children. There are rumors spreading like wildfire through the city," Gabriel said.

"What rumors?" Michael asked.

"There are two men going around preaching the word," Gabriel said. "I have seen them with my own eyes, old homeless men by the name of Moses and Elijah, but they are being hunted. Damien won't stand for this."

"I will go and find them," Anastasia said.

"No!" Michael snapped. "We will wait here, they will come to us." Anastasia watched them return to the building.

That night she sat silently on the window seal staring at the stars outside. She glanced back feeling someone watching her. She smiled, seeing Gabriel at the door. He slowly pulled a rose from behind his back. He walked over to her and sat down in front of her. She took the rose and smiled. They both looked outside and sighed. "The stars are bright tonight," Gabriel said. Anastasia nodded. "I miss home," Gabriel said. Anastasia looked over at him.

"We'll go back one day," she said. Gabriel looked over at her. "We'll see the waterfalls, the gardens, and see our father," Anastasia said. Gabriel smiled. They glanced back and saw the teens standing at the door. They smiled as the four teens raced over to them.

"We have to show you something," the young girl said, pulling Gabriel along with her. Anastasia followed them from the room.

Entering the church they saw the members of the families working on repairing the walls and floors. Gabriel walked over and helped one of the men lift the bench and slide it forward. Raphael and the others entered and joined in the rebuilding of the church.

Michael helped the two men lift the altar and set it in place. Anastasia stepped back and smiled seeing the church begin to come alive. Michael stepped back and stared at the church and nodded. "Pretty soon we can bring in the Christians and allow them to stay here," he said. "They would be protected here," he continued. Anastasia glanced back seeing movement inside the building. She quickly hurried from the sanctuary and looked around.

The first floor was empty. Walking over to the steps she looked up the stairs worried that someone who worked for Damien had made their way upstairs and was in the process of contacting him. She walked up the steps and came to the second floor. Looking around she had spotted no one. Behind her two elderly men stood. She jerked back and gasped seeing the two men watching her. "Elijah? Moses?" she said. The men stood silently. "What are you doing here?" Anastasia asked.

"The signs of end are near," Moses said. A red shadow passed through the curtains of the room. Anastasia entered the room and pulled back the lace window curtains. The dark blood red moon appeared in the sky. She glanced back at Moses and Elijah. "Tomorrow there will be a call, a call for all men, young and old, for their place will be on the battlefield," Moses said. Anastasia looked back at the moon then turned back to Elijah and Moses. They were now gone. Looking back she watched the stars slowly fade from the dark sky.

Damien watched from the window of the White House. He stared at the moon in anger. Quickly he shut the curtains and made his way past the desk and into the hallway. Several people followed him. "I want every building searched. I want all of them by tomorrow!" he snapped. The followers nodded. "Where are my soldiers?" he asked wondering why he had not seen his two marines for several days.

"They did not return," one lady said. "The crosses had not been removed from the cemetery."

"What???" Damien snapped.

"But don't worry, I had it taken care of," she said.

"Oh Delilah you're always wanting to please me," Damien said. Delilah smiled. "You will have the treasures of many," Damien said as he continued down the hall. She smiled and continued behind him with the others. He walked outside and stopped, seeing people in the streets. "Thank you all for coming tonight!" He called as the people cheered. "It is time we have all nations join our great nation. We become one, together we will live under one ruler! And that is I!" he called. The people cheered and applauded him. "There are things we must do to secure our wellbeing and that is to get rid of the distractions. The Christians have caused this division between us and we must no longer let them divide us. We must fight them!" he called. The crowd continued to cheer. "Tomorrow we will destroy everything they hold dear, we will take back this land and we will prevail!" He smiled as he looked to the back of the crowd and saw Anastasia standing silently at the gate of the White House. Her dress was covered in blood. Slowly blood drained from a wound to her head. His smile faded as she slowly pointed at him. "No!" he shouted.

Anastasia jerked awake in her bed and sat up. She breathed heavily as she pulled back the curtain and stared at the red moon in the sky. She slowly touched her forehead but didn't feel any wounds or signs of bleeding. "Must have been a bad dream," Gabriel said. She looked over at him sitting on the window seal of the second window.

"Something's going to happen to Damien," she said. "They don't see how bad he truly is. But this… this will show them. After this…they will fear him. But that power will be his." Gabriel slowly rose from the window seat.

"I have something to show you," he said. Anastasia slowly rose and followed him from the room.

They came down to the entrance to the church and stopped. "What is it?" Anastasia asked.

"Shut your eyes," Gabriel said. Anastasia smiled and shut her eyes as Gabriel opened the door and led her inside. "Okay, open them," he said. Anastasia opened her eyes and gasped as she looked around the newly built church. "How do you like it?" Gabriel asked.

"It's beautiful!" she said. She walked down the aisle and slowly slid her fingers across the wooden benches. She stopped at the altar and stared at the cross on the wall. Slowly she knelt down. Gabriel knelt down beside her. "It feels good to have a place to worship," she said. Gabriel smiled and nodded. The golden candles lit the church in a golden light around them. Anastasia slowly pulled out a Bible and laid it across her lap. Gabriel looked down at the Bible as they read it. Michael stood at the doors as he watched. He smiled as the two of them read it together. Slowly he moved away from the door as their voices echoed through the building.

Morning light slowly came through the stained glass windows of the Church. Anastasia slowly opened her eyes and lifted her head. She was laying on the soft carpet of the center aisle of the Church. Gabriel was laying asleep on the bench. Anastasia shut the Bible and rose. She walked over to the stain glass window and stared at the picture of Jesus hanging on the cross. The sound of cars making their way down the driveway alerted her. She quickly raced over to Gabriel. "Get up!" she said frantically. They raced from the church and shut the doors behind them. Michael and Raphael were running down the steps as the cars were pulling up front. Michael knelt beside the window and glanced out as several men got out of the cars and looked up at the building. They looked at one another then slowly stepped up the steps. They knocked on the doors as Anastasia walked over to the doors and pressed her palms against the wood. She shut her eyes then looked at the doors. Michael looked at her. She nodded as Michael rose and took the doorknob.

He slowly opened the doors as the two soldiers looked at him. "My name is Brandon, this is Danny," Brandon said. "We were ordered to get rid of the crosses and burn the flags," he said. "But we couldn't, we were told that we could take refuge here." There were the sounds of more doors closing outside. Several more soldiers walked up the steps. Anastasia smiled as she looked at Michael. Michael stepped outside as at least fifteen more people came up the doors.

"Word spreads fast," Michael said.

"Those elderly men can't keep their mouth shuts apparently," Danny said. Anastasia and Gabriel smiled. Michael nodded as Raphael opened the second door.

"Our home is yours," Michael said allowing them to enter. They watched as at least fifteen people entered the building, many were soldiers that had found the dishonor of their new leader and had fled.

The soldiers sat at the table eating as Michael leaned against the counters. "I was told to remove the crosses," Danny said. "But how could I? My father's grave was at the cemetery, and he had a cross on his head stone," he said. "I couldn't do it."

"He had me bring him the American Flag and he burnt it in a trash can," Brandon said. "Along with my medal I earned in war. No leader would do that. No leader that I follow." Raphael shook his head as he walked over to the counter and stood beside Michael.

"The days are growing dark in the east. The people are unsettled," he said.

"These elderly men talked about a war. Is there a war coming?" Brandon asked.

"There is," Michael said. "It's your choice if you want to fight in it or not," he continued. Brandon looked at Danny then at Michel.

"I'll fight in it," he said. Michael nodded.

"You're young and strong, I have no doubt in my heart that you could handle the battle, but I will not ask you to do so," he said.

"But I fought in many battles since the 9/11 attacks on the World Trade Centers," Brandon said.

"How old are you?" Raphael asked.

"Twenty five," Brandon said. Danny looked at Brandon then at Michael.

"He's a strong soldier. You would be pleased to have him at your side in battle," Danny said.

"That I do not doubt but…this war will be long and very hard," Michael said. "What you are up against…." Michael shook his head. "You will not survive it."

"I beg your pardon, but I've fought in the middle-east I know what it is like," Brandon said. "Have you?"

Michael glared at him. "I have fought in far many battles then you could ever imagine. I have fought against my own brother," Michael snapped back at him. "I watched my brother fall at my hands and I saw his army follow him. So don't speak to me about war sir, you do not know your place." Brandon became quiet and returned to his seat. "Finish eating, I need to talk to you guys about Damien," Michael said.

"About who?" Danny asked.

"Damien," Michael said. Danny and Brandon looked at one another.

"We do not know a Damien," Danny said in confusion.

"But you know Mason," Raphael said. Danny and Brandon looked at one another then at Raphael.

"Yes, he's the new leader that took over," Danny said. Brandon agreed.

"He's no longer your leader," Michael said. Danny and Brandon frowned.

"What?" he asked.

"His name is Damien," Michael said.

"I'm confused," Brandon said shaking his head.

"It's hard to explain…but you have to trust us on this," Michael said.

"Are you a cop?" Danny asked seeing Michael's police coat on the chair.

"I was before the rapture," Michael said.

"So you believe that this new leader is different than the leader that first took over?" Brandon asked in confusion.

"Yes," Raphael said.

"Well he did seem a bit on edge," Danny said with a nod. "If he's not our leader, who is he?"

"His name is Damien, he's the anti-Christ," Michael said. Danny stared at him.

"The one the Bible talks about?" he asked.

"The Bible only describes him as the beast," Raphael said.

"So he's like a monster?" Brandon asked.

"On the inside," Gabriel said.

"So…he's like possessed?" Brandon asked. Michael nodded. "Why not take the monster out?" Brandon asked.

"Easier said than done," Raphael responded.

"Damien won't give up that easily," Michael said.

"You're talking about a demon being inside of him?" Brandon said. "I mean get a priest or something."

"You can't take him out," Michael said. "He won't go."

"Then what do we do?" Brandon asked.

"We wait," Michael said.

"For what exactly?" Danny asked.

"We take him to war," Gabriel said.

"You mean…fight against him in battle?" Danny asked. "I mean this is end of the world type stuff." Michael, Raphael and Gabriel stared at him. Danny remained silent as he stared at them. "Are you terrorists?" he asked.

"No," Michael said smiling as he shook his head. "We're warriors."

"Like ninjas?" Brandon asked. Gabriel smiled as he laughed softly. Michael looked over at him. Instantly Gabriel became silent as Michael squeezed his arm.

Danny rose slowly. "Look, I'm a soldier, my duty is to protect my people," he said.

"As is mine," Michael said.

"You're a cop," Danny said.

"So you think," Michael said. "I'm…" he fell silent as he looked over at Raphael and Gabriel. He turned back to Danny.

"What do you know of war?" Danny asked.

"He's a commander, a leader, he's the head of the army that will take down your leader," Gabriel said. "You should show him some respect." Michael glared back at Gabriel. He slowly gave a nod knowing that Gabriel was just trying to help. He looked back at Danny.

"My army is gathering, your leader will call war upon my army and when he does we will strike him down," Michael said.

"So you're against us," Danny said.

"No, I'm protecting you and your people from being destroyed," Michael said.

"Just show him," Anastasia said entering the room.

"Show me what?" Danny asked. "What are you hiding?"

"I have to trust you first that you will honor your code as a soldier," Michael said.

"I've always held that honor. My father was a veteran as am I, so is Brandon. If someone is trying to destroy everything we stand for, we will fight," Danny said with a nod.

"What I'm about to show you must stay between us," Michael said. Danny nodded. Michael led Danny, Raphael, Brandon and Gabriel down the hall and up the steps.

Danny entered the empty room and stopped. "You're showing me an empty room?" he asked. Michael walked over to the wall and pressed his palm against the wall. Slowly the walls moved apart to reveal weapons. Danny and Brandon looked around the room in shock. "What on earth?" Danny whispered walking over to a wall of daggers and swords. He turned back to Michael. "These weapons, they haven't been used in war for many years, decades even," Danny said. "Who are you guys?"

"We're your leader's worst enemy," Raphael said.

"So you're coming at him with swords and daggers? Good luck with that," Brandon said. Brandon and Danny begin to leave the room.

"Try with an entire army," Michael said. Danny and Brandon stopped and looked back at him.

"They will blow you up so fast," Danny said. "Even the strongest army cannot stand against them."

"God's army can," Michael said.

"God's army?" Danny said returning to the room. "So…you're their leader huh? You expect us to believe that?"

"Believe what you want," Michael said pressing his palm against the wall and the walls close. "But when the trumpet sounds, war will come. Decide which side you're going to fight on."

"I've already decided," Brandon said.

"That you have," Michael said walking from the room. Danny looked over at Brandon.

"So you're just going to walk away from this?" he asked.

"You believe them?" Brandon asked.

"The man has weapons stashed in the walls, he has a Church downstairs," Danny said. "I wouldn't have believed it if I hadn't seen it. I do not trust this new leader in that White House. This man I trust." Brandon nodded.

"I trust you," he said. "If you trust him, so do I." Danny nodded and patted his shoulder.

In the kitchen Michael laid a map across the table as everyone gathered around. "Now, I know some of you know where more Christians are hiding, we go in at night and we bring them here," Michael said.

"It won't be easy to get them out with guards around," he said. "Guards will be standing at different corners," he said pointing to different buildings on the map.

"That's why we do it in shifts," Michael said.

"Reminds me of the Underground Railroad," Raphael said. Michael looked over at him. "The guards will not be kind," Raphael said. "If you are caught, you will be killed."

"That's why you have to move quickly and make no sounds," Michael said. The others nod. "We move out at dusk," Michael said folding the map.

That evening Anastasia sat on the marble bench in the garden. Gabriel slowly appeared at the gate and held up a white rose. Anastasia smiled as Gabriel walked over and sat down beside her. "So…" she began to take the rose and smell it. "So you're going with them?" she asked.

"I have to," Gabriel said. "You can't protect me."

Anastasia smiled. "I know," she said. Gabriel smiled. "Do you trust them?" Anastasia asked as they watched the soldiers walk out to the van.

Gabriel watched them and then slowly nodded. "I do," he said. "Do you not?"

"I don't know," Anastasia said. She looked down at the rose as the wind blew gently. She sighed and slowly stood as Gabriel looked up at her.

"Follow me," he said. Anastasia smiled and followed him down the brick path through the dead garden. They come to another stone wall. Anastasia stared at the gates and looked over at Gabriel.

Gabriel forced open the gate leading to another garden and led Anastasia into it. Anastasia glanced around slowly to the plants that were now alive. Different flowers are in flower beds and the trees are bright green as they sway in the breeze. Birds are sitting in the birdbath splashing. Gabriel laughed as he pointed them out. Anastasia laughed. "Come with me," Gabriel said racing down the pathway. Anastasia followed him. They raced across the stone walk way and through the small stream. They came to a stop in front of a water fountain that was surrounded by a marble bench. There was a figure of Mary pouring water into the fountain. Anastasia walked over and sat down on the bench and slid her fingers across the water as Gabriel sat down in front of her. Slowly she slid her finger across Gabriel's brow and down between his eyes. "For protection. Only true Christians can see the cross," she said. Gabriel slowly dipped his finger into the water did the same on her forehead. He took her hand and slowly kissed it.

"Gabriel, we must go," Michael called. Gabriel and Anastasia rose. Gabriel smiled and quickly hurried down the pathway and disappeared. Anastasia looked back at the statue of Mary and watched tears of blood coming down her face. Slowly she looked down at what once was a white rose, was now red.

CHAPTER NINE

Gabriel sat in the back of the large truck with Michael. He watched the building disappear behind the large gates. Michael looked over at him "Don't let human feelings overwhelm you," he said. Gabriel looked over at him. Michael slowly traced the cross on Gabriel's forehead. "A sign of God's power," he said. "In the end all that believe will have it," he said.

"Will it save them from the wrath of Damien?" Gabriel asked. Michael smiled.

"It will only be seen by Christians," he said. Gabriel nodded as the truck bounced along the dark road. "Do not worry my brother, for we will rejoice in his kingdom." Gabriel smiled and looked back at the building in the far distances.

Anastasia raced down the hall and threw open the doors to the Church and raced up to the altar and knelt down. "Forgive them father!" she whispered as she prayed. "The people of the city they do not know what is coming," she said. She felt two men watching her from behind. She glanced back slowly and saw the two elders. Rising, she watched them. "Elijah! Moses!" she said running to them and kneeling down at their feet.

"Rise child," Moses said taking her hands. "Good things are to come. For it is God's will." Anastasia took a Bible from the bench and handed it to Moses. Moses took it and tucked it under his arm. Elijah took the Bible as Anastasia handed him another one. "The Gospel will spread like fire in the brush, no land will be left untouched," Moses said. Anastasia watched the two leave the church. She raced from the church and stopped, seeing that they were now gone. She looked back at the altar and sighed.

The night had over taken the city as Raphael pulled into the city and stopped the truck. Michael and Gabriel slid down and looked around for any signs of people or guards watching. They motioned for the others to come. They quickly hurried over to the building and watched from the shadow. Michael watched the White House in the distance. There were no signs of guards around. He quickly motioned the others to go while he kept guard. They quickly made their way down the street. "Check for boarded windows," Raphael said. Gabriel knelt down and saw the boarded windows. He quickly hurried down the steps to the lower part of the building. He knocked softly. He could hear movement on the other side of the door.

"I'm here to help," he whispered between the cracks in the door. "We have a safety area you can go." Slowly the lock on the door clicked as a man appeared. "Come with us for your safety, bring whoever is with you," Gabriel said. The man stared at the cross on Gabriel's forehead. He nodded.

Raphael and the two soldiers helped at least five people to the truck. The people quickly climbed in as Michael continued to watch the area. He glanced back as another three people climbed into the truck. He looked forward as two guards made their way down the street. "Guards!" he whispered, looking back. Gabriel, Raphael and everyone got down as the guards walked towards them. Michael watched five more guards walk down the street towards the other two. He groaned and looked back at them. Gabriel watched him. Michael shook his head, warning him not to interfere if he was taken. Raphael slowly climbed into the passenger side and slid over to the driver's side as they quickly got in. Brandon watched Michael as he remained beside the truck.

"Get in!" Gabriel said, holding out his hand. Brandon shook his head.

"Don't be stupid!" Danny said. Brandon watched the guards as they got closer. Danny held out his hand. "Brandon, let's go!" he said. Brandon held out his hand as Danny pulled him into the truck.

"Hey!" one of the guards called. They walked quickly towards the truck with their hands on their guns. Raphael and Gabriel stared at the guards. "Get them!" the guard shouted. The guards began to run towards the truck. Michael sighed heavily as he leaned against the brick building. The ground rumbled as the guards stopped and aimed their guns at the truck. They fired, but the guns clicked but no gunshots went off. They stared at the guns as Michael stepped out from behind the building.

In the White House, oval office, Damien rose from his chair as he stared back at the window. "Michael," he frowned. He quickly grabbed his coat and made his way from the office. Several guards walked with him down the hall towards the door. Michael and the guards entered the White House. Damien stopped. "Well…isn't this a sight to see," he said. Michael was in handcuffs surrounded by guards. "You gave up that easy?" Damien said.

"Not much of a choice," Michael said.

"Where are the others? He usually has two others with him," Damien said.

"They got away," one of the guards said. Damien looked at the guard.

"I'm sorry? Did I hear you correctly? They got away?" he snapped.

"Yes sir," the guard said. Damien stared at the guard. The guard cringed as he slowly removed his gun from his belt. Michael looked at him, then at Damien.

"Please, spare his life," he pleaded. Damien looked at him.

"In return for what?" Damien said. Michael sighed heavily. Damien smiled. "That's what I thought," he said as he looked at the guard. He nodded as the guard held a gun under his own chin.

"Take me instead," Michael said, hoping to spare the guards life.

"You would give your life to save this human?" Damien asked.

"Yes," Michael said.

"You have become much more attached than I would have thought," Damien snapped angrily. "They are nothing but filthy humans and what would you do for them? Give your own life?"

"If it came to that," Michael said. Damien laughed.

"I can't believe it Michael, one of the greatest angels, God's commander in chief, in my house," he said. "It's a shame really, someone as wise as you. Willing to give his life for these people. Take him the prison," Damien said. "Find those that got away."

The guards nodded and led Michael down the hall. "I want them all dead!" Damien called as he returned to his office.

Back at the church, Gabriel raced over to the horse in the small garage. He grabbed the saddle and placed it on the back of the horse. Anastasia entered the garage. "You can't do this!" she said. Gabriel buckled the girth to the saddle.

"I have no choice," he said tightening tightening the girth. Anastasia walked over to him.

"It's what he wanted," she said.

"I don't believe that," Gabriel said.

"Why was he the lookout then?" Anastasia said. Gabriel looked over at her. "He wanted to make sure you guys got away," Anastasia said. She gripped his hand. "I assure you, he will not go down without a fight." "I know what he is planning," Gabriel said. "He's leaving to go to the Middle East. It's mine and Raphael's job to follow."

"Then I cannot stop you," Anastasia said. Gabriel looked over at her. "Jared and I must stay to help those here." Gabriel nodded.

"I understand," he frowned as he squeezed her hand. "We will meet again," he said. Gabriel quickly placed the bridle on the horse. He turned back as Raphael appeared with his horse.

"Are we ready?" Raphael asked. Gabriel nodded. He turned back to Anastasia and smiled.

"When the war ends we will have a great celebration. There's so much to look forward to," he said. Anastasia smiled. Slowly Gabriel placed the shawl around his shoulders and placed the hood over his head. Anastasia placed a cross and dove pendant on his shawl. Gabriel smiled.

"Thank you," he said. Anastasia smiled as he slowly placed two small daggers on the holders around his boots. He climbed unto the saddle and grabbed the reins. He rode the horse from the garage. Raphael and his men quickly followed. She watched them disappear into the darkness, knowing this could be the last time she would see them until after the war.

Then morning came. In the jail Michael sat listening to people sobbing and some cursing. He looked over at a sixteen-year-old boy sitting along in a cell. "What are you here for?" he asked. The boy looked over at him slowly.

"I was reading the Bible," he whispered. "My parents were taken in the rapture and I had been living with my uncle since then, I didn't know he was secretly working for the government," he said.

"He turned you in?" Michael asked. The boy nodded. "What's your name?"

"Preston," the boy answered.

"Do not fear, Preston, God will rule over all," Michael said.

"You're a Christian?" Preston asked.

Michael nodded. "God is my creator." Preston smiled.

"What will they do to me?" he asked.

"I don't know," Michael said. "But whatever they do, just know that God will take care of you," he said. Preston nodded as the sound of door opening could be heard. The screams and cries filled the prison as guards made their way down the hall. The guards stepped up front of Preston's cell. They opened the gates and pulled him from the cell and unto the floor. They took the chains off his wrist and yanked him back up. Michael watched the guards place a noose around Preston's neck. "No! No! Take me!" Michael called. The guards slammed the baton against the cell bars knocking Michael back. Preston looked at him in fear. The guards led him from the prison. Michael sat leaning against the prison bars watching in heartbreak as the boy was led outside.

Gabriel, Raphael and the other angels raced over to the back of the building and looked around the corner as steam slowly rose from manhole covers. An ear-piercing scream could be heard as the sound of hooves racing down the pavement came through the steam. A horse and guard charged down the alley at a fast rate of speed. Gabriel gasped seeing a young teen being dragged down the street behind it. The screams continued as the horses charged into the center of the city where thousands were gathered, cheering. Gabriel,

Raphael, and the others hurried over to the nearby building and watched as the guard on the horse slid down. The guard walked back to the teen who was now covered in blood and had shattered knees and ankles. The teenager screamed in agony as he was pulled to his feet and dragged up the steps to a platform where several guards waited. They held him up by his arms as the angry crowd cheered. Several men in the front threw rocks at him striking him in the face and chest. The guards pulled the boy over to the noose and strapped it around his neck. The boy sobbed as he struggled to hold up his head.

Gabriel watched him as the boy looked over at him pleadingly. Slowly Gabriel pulled the hood over his head and stepped out from the building. "What are you doing?" Raphael called. Gabriel stepped into the crowd and walked through them as he made his way to the front. The boy stared down at him as Gabriel stopped in front of the people. Preston continued to stare down at him as blood drained down his face. Gabriel glanced back as Preston looked up at the White House. Damien stood at the gates watching the public execution taking place. Suddenly a gunshot rang out from a building close by. The people in the crowd began to run for cover as more shots could be heard.

Damien gasped as Gabriel stood in the crowd watching him. "GET HIM!" he shouted. Gabriel held up his hand as a cloud of dust came between him and the crowd. "Find him now!" Damien shouted. The guard on the platform quickly ran towards Gabriel reaching ahead of them. He stopped as Gabriel looked at him. Slowly the guard broke down and fell to his knees as he sobbed. Gabriel stepped up on the platform. The boy looked at Gabriel in pain and agony as he fought back tears.

"Who are you?" he asked as Gabriel knelt down.

"A friend," Gabriel said. He knew there was no chance to save the boy. The boy sobbed as he clutched as Gabriel's hands. "Be not afraid," he said. He pressed his hand over the boy's eyes. The boy became silent and laid across the platform. Gabriel slowly rose and looked back at the guard. The guard remained on his knees.

"I'm sorry! I'm sorry! Please!" the guard begged. Gabriel stepped down from the platform. The guard rose as Gabriel walked up to him. The guard shook his head as he looked at the blood on his hands. "My wife was among the Christians when they were raptured. I am lost," he begged as he fell on his knees in front of Gabriel. "I killed that boy!" he shouted as his body shook from the sobs. Gabriel took his hands and pulled him to his feet.

"It is not too late to be saved," he said.

"What do I do?" the guard asked. Gabriel looked into the man's eyes.

"You ask Christ into your heart," he said as he watched the man pull a Bible from inside his police vest, "and when you have received him as your savior…" Gabriel continued, handing him a piece of paper. The guard opened the piece of paper and saw the instructions on how to become saved.

"This is all I do?" the guard asked.

"No," Gabriel said as he watched the people race down the street in every direction. "You have to believe in him with all your heart," Gabriel said. "You have to believe that Christ died for you." The guard nodded. "And when you do, you will know what to do next."

Brandon and Danny walked over and stood beside the platform. The guard looked down at the paper in his hands and over at Brandon and Danny as they walked over to him.

Gabriel entered the prison and stopped, seeing hundreds of people in prison cells. Michael looked over at him. Gabriel raced over to the jail cell and pulled on the lock. "There are keys!" Michael called. Gabriel looked around and spotted the keys in a locked box. He raced over to the box and smashed the glass, and grabbed the keys. The sounds of the horse hooves could be heard outside the prison. Gabriel struggled to unlock the lock as smoke began to rise from under the door. Finally the lock opened. The door opened as flames began to consume the building. Damien entered the building as flames rose around him.

Michael walked from his cell and forced Gabriel back as Damien stood silently with a smile.

"You won't get away that fast," he said. Gabriel looked at Michael then at Damien. "You know that was a nice trick with the whole dust storm," Damien said. "But don't think I didn't see what you did, boy." Damien smiled and shook his head as people in the prison cells screamed as fire began to consume the building. "I can stand here all day if I wish and the fire won't hurt me a bit!" He said. "Well, maybe the outer shell, but in the end, my master will be satisfied." Michael watched Damien as they stood silently.

"This war will come from all sides, from every corner of the world," Michael snapped.

"I do agree my brother," Damien said. "I hope you have your army ready. Because we won't back down."

"They're ready and waiting," Michael said. Suddenly a gunshot sounded and the buzz of a bullet going past Michael's ear caused him to jerk away. The bullet struck Damien in the head. He gasped as he collapsed to his knees. Michael and Gabriel glanced back and saw Danny with a gun in his hand. Michael stared back at Damien. "Free the people. Go!" Michael demanded as he shoved Gabriel forward. Michael looked back at Danny. Tears stream down his face as he slowly dropped the gun. Michael walked over to him. "Go," Michael said.

"I had to kill him," Danny said.

"You didn't kill him," Michael said.

"I shot him in the head," Danny said.

"He will arise, and after he does they will see his true side," Michael said. "Help my brother free these people," he said. Danny nodded and raced over to the prisoners as Michael watched Damien lay on the ground.

At the church building Anastasia sat up hearing a gunshot in her dream. She quickly threw back the covers and rose from the bed. Racing down the steps she quickly raced to the church doors and raced inside. Kneeling at the altar she folded her hands and looked up at the cross. One of Raphael's men named Tim, rushed into the church. Rising, Anastasia looked back at him. "We have more people coming," Tim said. Anastasia nodded.

"The gunshot?" she asked.

"Danny shot him," Tim said.

"So they know?" Anastasia asked.

"The prisoners don't, but they will soon enough," Tim said. People began to file into the church. Some were startled and in a deep state of shock from what they had witnessed. Raphael and two other men entered behind them filling the benches from the back to the front. Anastasia quickly hurried past the people and over to him.

"Gabriel? Michael?" she asked.

"They're both fine," Raphael said.

"Damien?" Anastasia asked. Raphael took her arm and led her into the church.

"They're reporting it all over the news, people believe he is dead," he said.

"What do we do?" Anastasia asked.

"Pray for peace and hope," Tim said. Anastasia nodded as Tim quickly raced from the church and helped the people that had just entered. Anastasia looked over at the altar and the cross, trying to keep herself calm. She sighed heavily as an elderly woman walked over to her and hugged her as she sobbed. Anastasia hugged her tightly praying that Christ would find his way among the people of the city.

CHAPTER TEN

The hospital doors flew open as the nurses and doctors pushed the stretcher down the long hallway. Blood was draining heavily from the gunshot wound to Damien's head. He was quickly brought into an empty room as guards surrounded the door that was packed with reporters and photographers. Michael walked down the hall and stood back and watched as the guards held back the photographers. Gabriel raced over to him, "They're all safe," he said. Michael nodded as he continued to watch the room. Gabriel stared at the room then at Michael. "It's just going to make people believe in him more," he said.

"I know," Michael said. "Where are the witnesses?"

"Last time I saw them they were preaching the Gospel outside the White House," Gabriel said. Michael looked over at him.

"Go and find them," Michael said. Gabriel nodded and raced from the hospital.

Out in the streets people were standing and listening to the news in fear as televisions in store windows are displaying the news about the attempted assassination of the leader. Gabriel stopped close by and looked at the screen showing the nurses and doctors working on Damien. He turned away and quickly hurried down the street. A large crowd had gathered around the two witnesses who were speaking about the gospel. Pushing his way through the crowd Gabriel stopped and saw that the crowd was now restless and shouting angrily at the two witnesses. Gabriel looked around slowly at the crowd. He looked over at the two witnesses as they looked at him. "The days to come will be many," Elijah said. The crowd shouted angrily. "War is among us," Elijah called.

"You lie!" a woman shouted throwing a stone at Elijah. Gabriel jumped, seeing the stone strike Elijah in the face. A large gash appeared across his cheek. A man raced into the crowd.

"He is dead!" He announced. The crowd glanced over at him. "Our leader is dead!" Gabriel looked back at the two witnesses. He walked over to them.

"Goodbye, my son," Moses whispered.

"Goodbye," Gabriel said. Elijah handed him a small Bible and frowned.

"He will return when the sky rolls back like a scroll," he said. Gabriel smiled as Elijah kissed his cheek. Gabriel slowly turned and walked through the crowd. The crowd turned back angrily to the two witnesses. Gabriel walked back over to Michael who was waiting at the hospital.

"You ready?" Michael asked. Gabriel looked at him and nodded. He slowly slid the Bible into his coat and walked with Michael down the street. Several gunshots could be heard coming from the crowd followed by cheers.

Anastasia stood in front of the television as Tim entered the room. The crowd of people had gathered beside her as they watched. Some sobbed as they watched the mistreatment of the two witnesses. Tim and Raphael's other men stood behind the crowd of people. Anastasia walked through the crowd and over to them. "We have to leave my lady," Raphael said. Anastasia nodded. Raphael forced a smile. "Watch for the signal, and when you see it let the others know it is time," he said. Anastasia nodded as Raphael handed her a cross carved out of wood. She smiled as she kissed his cheek.

"For safety," she said. Raphael smiled.

"In three days allow the people to awaken and see," Raphael said. Anastasia nodded. "The witnesses will be brought here, one of these men is a reporter and he has a camera man with him make sure he is recording, and when he does, the world will see God's almighty power," he said.

"And the leader?" Anastasia asked.

"Let us take care of that," Raphael replied.

"Take care of them," she said. Raphael nodded.

"Don't worry, Michael will not allow any of his men to take a fall," he answered. Anastasia watched as Raphael and his men grabbed their bags and walked from the building.

Anastasia raced outside as the men got in the truck. They looked over at her with forced smiles. Anastasia smiled back as the truck drove down the long driveway towards the main road into the city. She walked back into the building and shut the door behind her.

Michael watched from the door, as Damien lay motionless on the stretcher. The doctor slowly covered his face with a white blanket. Gabriel walked over to Michael and stood beside him. "The witnesses are dead," he said.

"I know," Michael said.

"Danny and Brandon are taking the bodies to the Church," Gabriel said. "Anastasia will know what to do."

"The bags of weapons?" Michael asked.

"I got them," Gabriel said. Michael looked back into the room.

"Are you sure we should leave so soon?" Gabriel asked. Michael nodded.

"It's time," he said. He walked away from the door and down the hall as Gabriel walked beside him. They stepped through the doors and stopped seeing Raphael and his men standing and waiting.

"Where to Commander?" Raphael asked.

"Babylon," Michael said. Raphael frowned as the men picked up the bags and followed Michael down the sidewalk.

Anastasia entered the church and watched several men lay the witnesses down on the front steps of the worship area. Slowly people entered the church and sat down in the seats. They stared heartbrokenly at the witnesses. "Who will tell us of this Jesus now?" one woman asked. Anastasia looked back at them. The worship area was now almost completely full, she looked back at the witnesses and sighed, knowing the time would be coming soon to show the people of the world God's power.

As the night progressed candles were lit around the church. Anastasia sat on the front seat watching the two witnesses. The smell of decaying bodies began to fill the church. Deep down her heart broke as she watched them lying there. It was a human emotion, something that she was not use to feeling but she could feel the emotions from the people around her. Slowly an elderly woman took her hand. "You're waiting on something," the lady said. Anastasia looked at her.

"Like what?" she asked.

"I don't know, I can't place my finger on it," the elderly lady replied. Anastasia smiled.

"Do you fear God?" she asked. The elderly woman smiled and nodded.

"I fear the power in which our God can place upon this world," she said, "for he is a powerful God. Without him I would have no hope … no hope for the future, and have no hope of my place in Heaven," the elderly lady said. Anastasia smiled.

"My son had cancer for two years before he passed," a man said. "The night before he died he told me that he saw a man in a white robe come to him in a dream," he said. "That's when I knew there was a God, I chose not to get saved and I regret that every day." Anastasia watched the people around watching and listening. The reporter stood slowly as his cameraman picked up the camera.

"People in this world may not believe in God but I do, if the leader in that hospital is our God then he wouldn't have allowed this to happen to us," another woman cried. Anastasia walked to the front of the church and slowly laid down several white roses beside the witnesses. She turned back to the crowd in the church.

"God is with us here," she began. "He will protect us." The elderly woman smiled as she looked at Anastasia. "In time we will be in his grace and in his kingdom. You see these witnesses? They are not dead but are sleeping," she said. "For when the time comes, they will awake and rise," she said. "For God is not a selfish God but a gracious God," she added. The people in the crowd nodded in agreement. Anastasia looked back at the elderly men lying on the steps.

As the three days passed, Anastasia sat in the garden watching the water in the fountain coming down. The elderly woman walked over to her and took her hands. Anastasia smiled and rose. "Tonight we worship," she said. Anastasia walked with her towards the gate of the garden. Anastasia stopped, and felt something watching her from behind. She turned back and saw a large white eagle sitting on the bench of the garden. It ruffled its' feathers as it glanced around. Anastasia smiled as she walked from the garden. The eagle flew into the woods and disappeared.

That night Anastasia sat on the bench in the church and watched the witnesses. The crowd had slept several nights on the benches fearing that if they step anywhere outside the church the guards would capture them. Danny and Brandon guarded the doors. Slowly Anastasia rose and walked from the church auditorium. Danny and Brandon looked over at her as she entered the kitchen. She returned with several cups of water. She offered the cups to them. "Thank you," Danny said.

"I'm going out to pray," Anastasia said. Danny nodded as he watched her walk outside.

Anastasia opened the gate of the garden and entered. She looked around at the flowers and plants. She stopped, feeling someone standing close by. Glancing back she smiled, seeing Gabriel standing along the garden wall. She hurried over and hugged him. "I thought you had left," she said.

"Not without a goodbye first," Gabriel said. Anastasia smiled. The white eagle landed on the bench close by and waited. "Tonight the people will see. They will know that our God is the true king," he said, gripping her hands.

"I do not fear it," Anastasia said.

Gabriel smiled as Anastasia handed him a white rose. "Thank you," Gabriel said. He slowly placed the rose inside his coat pocket. "It will be long, but it's worth the fight. It's worth everything we have ever known. In the morning Danny and Brandon will join us."

"I know," Anastasia said. "Take care of yourself okay?"

"I will," Gabriel said. He slowly pulled away and walked from the garden. Anastasia looked over at the eagle. It flew from the bench and followed Gabriel. She raced over to the bench and knelt down and folded her hands and looked up at the sky.

"Lord, help these people to understand," she whispered. "I cannot do this alone." Lightening flashed brightly through the sky and ended with a loud crash of thunder. Anastasia rose as she walked from the garden.

Several nurses cleaned the head wound of Damien. They looked down at him sadly. Sobbing they laid the wash clothes down in the bowl. Slowly his fingers curled around the bed sheets. The nurses stepped back as Damien's chest began to rise and fall. Damien gasped as the head wound healed. He jerked awake and sat up on the stretcher startling the nurses. The nurses jerked back with a scream as Damien sat up on the bed and looked around. He watched as the nurses raced from the room in horror. Looking over at the machine he smiled, seeing the pulse beating again. Looking forward, he watched several doctors enter the room. "Good evening gentlemen," he said.

After several hours of confusion Damien sat in the hospital bed as people from the White House gathered around him, happy that he was alive, but confused at what had happened. "How did this happen? I don't understand," his secretary asked.

Damien smiled. "It's a miracle that's what," he said. He looked over at a reporter who was standing beside the cameraman. "I want to thank everyone for the well wishes," he said. "I'm happy to be here, alive," he said. The secretary smiled.

"It really is a miracle, there certainly is a God and he is here," she said. Damien smiled and nodded.

"He is," he said.

Back at the church Danny, Brandon and the others of the church watched the television screen. "How could this be? He is certainly not God!" One woman called.

"I shot him in the head!" Danny snapped. "I don't get this." The elderly woman shook her head.

"There must be a mistake," she said. She returned to the church and stopped seeing the witnesses still lying on the steps. The people returned to their seats as they watched.

"If God is so powerful and he is there for us, then where is he?" one man asked.

"We must be patient," the elderly lady said.

"I'm tired of being patient," a man shouted. Suddenly the church doors are thrown open by a violent burst of wind. The cameraman rose and held his camera as Anastasia entered the church and walked down the aisle. The people of the church watched in horror as lightening flashed outside. The candles blew out and the church became dark. Kneeling, Anastasia watched the cross as the light surrounded it.

"Show this on every channel," the reporter said to his cameraman. The cameraman nodded. Anastasia rose slowly as light pierced through the windows. Slowly the witnesses began to breathe. The men and women of the church rose in shock as the elderly men began to move. Slowly they rose and stood on the steps as Anastasia rose. She turned back as she watched the shocked expressions of the people of the church. One by one the men and women of the church begun to kneel as Anastasia stepped down the steps with the two witnesses behind her. The elderly woman smiled as tears streamed down her face.

"This was done by my God," she said as she clutched the Bible to her chest. "He is alive!" she called. The men and women of the church held their hands up as the worshipped. Danny and Brandon fell to their knees as Anastasia and the two witnesses walked from the church.

At the hospital the secretary raced into the room and turned on the television. "You have to see this!" she said. Damien stared at the screen as he watched the witnesses rise on the steps.

"No! No!" he shouted ripping the bandages from his arms. "Turn it off!" He rose and raced from the room. He stopped as he watched every screen as they were turned to the newscast being reported from the church. "Find them! Kill them all!" he shouted. Guards raced down the hall. He looked back at his staff. "They are committing witchcraft!" he snapped. "We will end it."

People all over the world stared at the screen as the witnesses walked from the church. "How is this happening?" One man asked his wife.

A group of people hiding in an abandoned people held hands and worshipped as they watched the screen.

Suddenly the world had been awakened by the power of God… a power that the world had so desperately needed during those times.

At the loading dock Michael picked up a newspaper and saw a picture, not of Damien but of the witnesses. Gabriel walked over to him and looked at the paper. "So, the world knows," he said. Michael agreed.

"They do, the war has just started," he said folding the paper and placing it in his bag. Gabriel walked over to Raphael and his men who were waiting at the docks.

"You know, as much as I hate war, I'm ready for this," Raphael said.

"As am I, brother," Michael said. The men grabbed the bags sitting on the pavement and placed them over their shoulders. Gabriel glanced back as the white eagle landed on the dock railing. He smiled and nodded as he walked up the ramp towards the large boat waiting to take them across the Atlantic Ocean to the Middle East. Danny and Brandon appeared on board as Tony, their friend from the house in the woods, appeared beside them.

"You guys have a strange way of giving me a message," Tony called to them pointing at the eagle. Michael smiled as he walked up the ramp towards them. "Welcome aboard gentlemen," Tony said as Michael and his men stepped on the boat. "Are you sure about this?" Tony asked. Michael sat his bag down and walked over to the railing of the boat.

"I'm sure," Michael said with a nod. Tony nodded and walked over to the engine. Gabriel and the other men stood beside Michael in the front of the boat. They were the only ones on board as the boat moved across the canal towards open sea. The men spread out around the railing as Michael and Gabriel stood in the center watching the open sea ahead. "We're in for rough days ahead," Michael said. Gabriel continued to watch silently.

"I have your back brother," he said. Michael looked over at him and nodded.

"I have your back as well," Michael replied.

"We're in this together," Raphael said with a nod as they stared ahead. Michael looked back forward at the dark clouds in the distances. He sighed knowing the battle of Armageddon had just begun. Slowly the boat continued across the ocean towards the battlefield that would give way to the most gruesome battle of all time, where men, demons, and angels would clash and the way for Christ to return would be made.

AUTHOR BIO

 Kara Stalnaker's love of writing began at a very young age. Ever since she started writing in the first grade it has been her hobby and passion. While she was in college majoring in English and Communications her advisor taught her the art of screenplay writing and she has written screenplays and other dramatic stories since then. Her goal is to one day see her books be made into films where she can share her Christian convictions both through the written word and on the large screen. Kara currently makes her home in North Carolina with her family. She is a teacher as well as a writer.

Other books by
Kara Stalnaker

The Rookie

The Crossroad Trilogy:

The Gathering (Book 1)
The Uprising (Book 2)
The Kingdom (Book 3)